P9-CCM-648

NOT TO DISTURB

BY THE SAME AUTHOR

Novels

The Comforters
Robinson
Memento Mori
The Ballad of
Peckham Rye
The Bachelors
The Prime of Miss Jean Brodie
The Girls of Slender Means
The Mandelbaum Gate
The Public Image
The Driver's Seat

Play

Doctors of Philosophy

Poetry

Collected Poems I

Criticism and biography

The Brontë Letters
John Masefield
Child of Light

Stories

Collected Stories I

MURIEL SPARK

Not to Disturb

NEW YORK / THE VIKING PRESS

Published in 1972 by The Viking Press, Inc.
625 Madison Avenue, New York, N.Y. 10022
SBN 670-51667-8
Library of Congress catalog card number: 73-178820
Printed in U.S.A.

NOT TO DISTURB

I

The other servants fall silent as Lister enters the room.

"Their life," says Lister, "a general mist of error. Their death, a hideous storm of terror. –I quote from *The Duchess of Malfi* by John Webster, an English dramatist of old."

"When you say a thing is not impossible, that isn't quite as if to say it's possible," says Eleanor who, although younger than Lister, is his aunt. She is taking off her outdoor clothes. "Only technically is the not impossible, possible."

"We are not discussing possibilities today," Lister says. "Today we speak of facts. This is not the time for inconsequential talk."

"Of facts accomplished," says Pablo the handyman.

Eleanor hangs her winter coat on a hanger.

"The whole of Geneva will be talking," she says.

"What about him in the attic?" says Heloise, the youngest maid whose hands fold over her round stomach as she speaks. The stomach moves of its own accord and she pats it. "What about him in the attic?" she says. "Shall we let him loose?"

Eleanor looks at the girl's stomach. "You better get out of the way when the journalists come," she says. "Never mind him in the attic. They'll be making enquiries of you. Wanting to know."

"Oh," says Heloise, holding her stomach. "It's the quickening. I could faint." But she stands tall, placid and unfainting, gazing out of the window of the servants' sitting-room.

"He was a very fine man in his way. The whole of Geneva got a great surprise."

"Will get a surprise," Eleanor says.

"Let us not split hairs," says Lister, "between the past, present and future tenses. I am agog for word from the porter's lodge. They should be arriving. Watch from the window." And to the pregnant maid he says, "Have you got out all the luggage?"

"Pablo has packed his bags already," says Heloise, swivelling her big eyes over to the handyman with only a slight turn of her body.

"Sensible," says Lister.

"Pablo is the father," Heloise declares, patting her stomach which quivers under her apron.

"I wouldn't be so sure of that," Lister says. "And neither would you."

"Well it isn't the Baron," says Heloise.

"No, it isn't the Baron," says Lister.

"It isn't the Baron, that's for sure," says Eleanor.

"The poor late Baron," says Heloise.

"Precisely," says Lister. "He'll be turning up soon. In the Buick, I should imagine."

Eleanor is putting on an apron. "Where's my carrot juice? Go and ask Monsieur Clovis for my carrot juice. My eyes have improved since I went on carrot juice."

"Clovis is busy with his contract," Lister says. "He left it rather late. I made mine with *Stern* and *Paris-Match* over a month ago. Now of course there's still the movie deal to consider, but you want to play it cool. Don't forget. Play it cool and sell to the highest bidder."

Clovis looks up, irritably, from his papers. "France, Germany, Italy, bid high. But don't forget in the long run that English is the higher-income language. We ought to coordinate on that point." He continues his scrutiny of documents.

"Surely Monsieur Clovis is going to prepare a meal tonight isn't he?" says Eleanor. She goes through the door to the kitchen. "Clovis!" she calls. "Don't forget my carrot juice will you?"

"Quiet!" says Clovis. "I'm reading the small print. The small print in a contract is the important part. You can get your own damn carrot juice. There's carrots in the vegetable store and there's the blender in front of you. You all get your own supper tonight."

"What about them?"

"They won't be needing supper."

Lister stands in the doorway, now, watching his young aunt routing among the vegetables for a few carrots which she presses between her fingers disapprovingly.

"Supper, never again," says Lister. "For them, supper no more."

"These carrots are soft," says Eleanor. "Heloise doesn't know how to market. She's out of place in a house this style."

"The poor Baroness used to like her," says Clovis, looking up from the table where he is sitting studying the fine print. "The poor Baroness could see no wrong in Heloise."

"I see no wrong in her, either," Eleanor says. "I only say she doesn't know how to buy carrots."

Heloise comes to join them at the kitchen door.

"It's quickening," she informs Clovis.

"Well it isn't my fault," says the chef.

"Nor me neither, Heloise," says Lister severely. "I always took precautions the times I went with you."

"It's Pablo," says the girl, "I could swear to it. Pablo's the father."

"It could have been one of the visitors," Lister says.

Clovis looks up from his papers, spread out as they are on the kitchen table. "The visitors never got Heloise, never."

"There were one or two," says Heloise, reflectively. "But it's day and night with Pablo when he's in the mood. After breakfast, even." She looks at her stomach as if to discern by a kind of X-ray eye who the father truly might be. "There was a visitor or two," she says. "I must say, there did happen to be a visitor or two about the time I caught on. Either a visitor of the Baroness or a visitor of the Baron."

"We have serious business on hand tonight, my girl, so shut up," says the chef. "We have business to discuss and plenty to do. Quite a vigil. Has anybody arrived yet?"

"Eleanor, I say keep a look out of the window," Lister orders his aunt. "You never know when someone might leave their car out on the road and slip in. They're careless down at the lodge."

Eleanor cranes her neck towards the window, still feeling the soft carrots with a contemptuous touch. "Here comes Hadrian; it's only Hadrian coming up the drive. These carrots are past it. Terrible carrots."

The footsteps crunch to the back of the house.

Hadrian the assistant chef comes in with a brief-case under his arm.

"Did you get out my cabin trunk?" he asks Heloise.

"It's too big, in my condition."

"Well get Pablo to fetch it, quick. I'm going to start my packing."

"What about him in the attic?" says Heloise. "We better take him up his supper or he might create or take one of his turns."

"Of course he'll get his supper. It's early yet."

"Suppose the Baron wants his dinner?"

"Of course he expected his dinner," Lister says. "But as things turned out he didn't live to eat it. He'll be arriving soon."

"There might be an unexpected turn of events," says Eleanor.

"There was sure to be something unexpected," says Lister. "But what's done is about to be done and the future has come to pass. My memoirs up to the funeral are as a matter of fact more or less complete. At all events, it's out of our hands. I place the event at about three a.m. so prepare to stay awake."

"I would say six o'clock tomorrow morning. Right on the squeak of dawn," says Heloise.

"You might well be right," says Lister. "Women in your condition are unusually intuitive."

"How it kicks!" says Heloise with her hand on her stomach. "Do you know something? I have a craving for grapes. Do we have any grapes? A great craving. Should I get a tray ready for him in the attic?"

"Rather early," says Lister looking at the big moon-faced kitchen clock. "It's only ten past six. Get your clothes packed."

The large windowed wall of the servants' hall looks out on a gravelled courtyard and beyond that, the cold mountains, already lost in the early darkening of autumn.

A dark green, small car has parked here by the side entrance. The servants watch. Two women sit inside, one at the wheel and one in the back seat. They do not speak. A tall person has just left the other front seat and has come round to the front door.

Lister waits for the bell to ring and when it does he goes to open the door:

A long-locked young man, fair, wearing a remarkable white fur coat which makes his pink skin somewhat radiant. The coat reaches to his boots.

Lister acknowledges by a slight smile, in which he uses his mouth only, that he recognises the caller well from previous visits. "Sir?" says Lister.

"The Baroness," says the young man, in the quiet voice of one who does not wish to spend much of it.

"She is not at home. Will you wait, sir?" Lister stands aside to make way at the door.

"Yes, she's expecting me. Is the Baron in?" sounds the low voice of the young man.

"We expect him back for dinner, sir. He should be in shortly."

Lister takes the white fur coat, glancing at the quality and kind of mink, and at its lining and label as he does so. Lister, with the coat over his arm, turns to the left, crosses the oval hall, followed by the young man. Lister treads across the *trompe-l'œil* chequered paving of the hall and the young man follows. He wears a coat of deep blue satin with darker blue watered silk lapels, trousers of dark blue velvet, a pale mauve satin shirt with a very large high collar and a white cravat fixed with an amethyst pin. Lister opens a door and stands aside. The young man, as he enters, says politely to Lister, "In the left-hand outer pocket, this time, Lister."

"Thank you, sir," says Lister, as he withdraws. He closes the door again and crosses the oval hall to another door. He opens it, hangs the white mink coat gently on one of a long line of coat-hangers which are placed expectantly in order on a carved rack. Lister then feels in the outer left-hand pocket of the coat, withdraws a fat, squat, brown envelope, opens it with a forefinger, half-pulls out a bundle of banknotes, calculates them with his eyes, stuffs them back into the envelope, and places the envelope in one of his own pockets, somewhere beneath his white jacket, at heart-level. Lister looks at himself in the glass above the wash-basin and looks away. He arranges the neat unused hand-towels with the crested "K" even more neatly, and leaves the cloak-room.

The other servants fall silent as Lister returns.

"Number One," says Lister. "He walked to his death most gingerly."

"Sex," muses Heloise.

Lister shudders. "The forbidden word," he says. "Let me not hear you say it again."

"It's Victor Passerat, waiting there in the library," says Heloise.

"Mister Fair-locks," says Eleanor, looking at the carrot juice which she has prepared with the blender.

"I never went with him," says Heloise. "I had the chance, though."

"Didn't we all?" says Pablo.

"Speak for yourself," says Clovis.

"Less talk," says Lister.

"Victor Passerat isn't the dad," says Heloise.

"He'd never have had it in him," said Pablo.

"Are you aware," says Eleanor to her nephew, "that two ladies are waiting outside in the car that brought the visitor?"

Lister glances towards the window but next he

goes to a large cupboard and, drawing up a chair, mounts it. He carefully, one by one, removes the neat jars of preserved fruit that are stacked there, ginger in gin, cherries in cognac, apple and pineapple, marmalades of several types, some of them capped and bottled with a home-made look, others, according to their shapes and labels, fetched in from as far as Fortnum and Mason in London and Charles's in New York. All these Lister carefully places on a side-table, assisted by Eleanor and watched by the others in a grave silence evidently due to the occasion. Lister removes a plank shelf, now bare of bottles. At the back of the cupboard is a wall-safe, the lock of which Lister slowly and respectfully opens, although not yet the door. He demands a pen, and while waiting for Hadrian the assistant cook to fetch it, he takes the envelope from his inner pocket, and counts the bank-notes in full view of the rest.

"Small change," he says, "compared with what is to come, or has already come, according as one's philosophy is temporal or eternal. To all intents and purposes, they're already dead although as a matter of banal fact, the night's business has still to accomplish itself."

"Lister's in good vein tonight," says Clovis, who has left the perusal of his contract to join the group. Meanwhile Hadrian returns, handing up the simple ballpoint pen to Lister.

Upstairs the shutters bang.

"The wind is high tonight," Lister says. "We might not hear the shots." He takes the pen and marks a sum on the envelope, followed by the date. He then opens wide the safe which is neatly stacked with various envelopes and boxes, some of metal, some of leather. He places the new package among the rest, closes the safe, replaces the wooden shelf, and, assisted by Eleanor and Heloise, puts the preserve-bottles back in their places. He descends from his chair, hands the chair to Hadrian, closes the cupboard door, and goes to the window. "Yes," he says, "two ladies waiting in the car, as well they might. Good night, ladies. Good night, sweet, sweet, ladies."

"Why did they pull up round the side instead of waiting in the drive?" says Heloise.

"The answer," says Lister, "is that they know their place. They had the courage to accompany their kinsman on his errand, but at the last little moment lacked the style which alone was necessary to save him. The Baron will arrive, and not see them, not enquire. Likewise the Baroness. No sense, for all their millions."

"With all that in there alone," says Heloise, still contemplating the closed cupboard wherein lies the wall-safe of treasure, "we could buy the Montreux Palace Hotel."

"Who needs the Montreux Palace?" says Hadrian.

"Think big," says Pablo the handyman, patting her around the belly.

"How it kicks!" she says.

"How like," says Lister, "the death wish is to the life-urge! How urgently does an overwhelming obsession with life lead to suicide! Really, it's best to be half-awake and half-aware. That is the happiest stage."

"The Baron Klopstocks were obsessed with sex," says Eleanor. She is setting places at the long servants' table.

"Sex is not to be mentioned," Lister says. "To do so would be to belittle their activities. On their sphere sex is nothing but an overdose of life. They will die of it, or rather, to all intents and purposes, have died. We treat of spontaneous combustion. One remove from sex, as in Henry James, an English American who travelled."

"They die of violence," says Clovis who has transferred to the butler's desk his papers and the contract and documents he has been studying closely for the past three-quarters of an hour. He sits with his back to the others, looks half over his shoulders. "To be precise, it is of violence that they shortly die."

"Clovis," says Eleanor, "would you mind giving an eye to the oven?"

"Where's my assistant?" says Clovis.

"Hadrian has gone down to the lodge," says Eleanor. "Gone to borrow a couple of eggs. Him in the attic hasn't had his supper yet."

"No eggs in the house?" says Clovis.

"There was too much else to arrange today," says Eleanor as she places five tiny silver bowls of salt at regular intervals along the table, carefully measuring the distance with her eye. "No marketing done."

"Things have gone to rack and ruin," says Lister, "now that the crisis has arrived. This house hitherto was run like the solar system."

"Cook your own damn dinner," says Clovis, bending closely over his documents.

"Don't you want any?" says Heloise. "I'll eat your share if you like, Clovis, I'm eating for two."

Clovis bangs down his fist, drops his pen, goes across to the large white complicated cooking stove, studies the regulator, turns the dial, opens the stove door, and while looking inside, with the other hand snaps his finger. Heloise runs with a cloth and a spoon and places them in Clovis's hand. Protecting his hand with the cloth Clovis partly pulls out a casserole dish. He hooks up the lid with the handle of the spoon, peers in, sniffs, replaces the lid, shoves the dish back and closes the oven door. Again, he turns the dial of the regulator. Then with the spoon-handle, he lifts the lids from the two pots which are simmering on top of the stove. He glances inside each and replaces the lids.

"Fifteen minutes more for the casserole. In seven minutes you move the pots aside. We sit down at half-past seven if we're lucky and they don't decide to dine before they die."

"No they won't eat," says Lister. "We can have our dinner in peace while they get on with the job."

From somewhere far away at the top of the house comes a howl and a clatter.

"I'll have a vodka and tonic," says Clovis, as he passes through the big kitchen and returns to his papers at the butler's desk.

"Very good," says Lister, looking round. "Any more orders?"

"Nothing for me. I had my carrot juice. I couldn't stomach a sherry, not tonight," says Eleanor.

"Nerves," says Lister, and has started to leave the kitchen when the house-telephone rings. He returns to answer it.

"Lister here," he says, and listens briefly while something in the telephone crackles into the room. "Very good," he then says into the telephone and hangs up. "The Baron," says he, "has arrived."

The Baron's great car moves away from the porter's lodge while the porter closes the gates behind it.

It slightly swerves to avoid Hadrian who is walking up the drive.

The porter, returning to the lodge, finds his wife hanging up the house-telephone in the cold hall. "Lister sounds like himself," she tells her husband.

"What the hell do you expect him to sound like?" says the porter. "How should he sound?"

"He was no different from usual," she says. "Oh, I feel terrible."

"Nothing's going to happen, dear," he says, suddenly hugging her. "Nothing at all."

"I can feel it in the air, like electricity," she says. He takes her arm, urging her into the warm sitting-room. She is young and small. She looks as if she were steady of mind but she says, "I think I am going mad."

"Clara!" says the porter. "Clara!"

She says, "Last night I had a terrible dream."

Cecil Klopstock, the Baron, has arrived at his door, thin and wavering. The door is open and Lister stands by it.

"The Baroness?" says the Baron, passively departing from his coat which slides over Lister's arm.

"No, sir, she hasn't arrived. Mr. Passerat is waiting."

"When did he come?"

"About half-past six, sir."

"Anyone with him?"

"Two women in the car. They're waiting outside."

"Let them wait," says the Baron and goes towards the library, across the black and white paving of the hall. He hesitates, half-turns, then says, "I'll wash in here," evidently referring to a wash-room adjoining the library.

"I thought it best," Lister says as he enters the servants' sitting-room, "to tell him about those two women waiting outside, perceiving as I did from his manner that he had already noticed them. —'Anyone with Mr. Passerat?' he said with his eye to me. 'Yes, sir,' I said, 'two ladies. They are waiting in the car.' Why he asked me that redundant question I'll never know."

"He was testing you out," says Hadrian who is whisking two eggs in a bowl.

"Yes, that's what I think, too," says Lister. "I feel wounded. I opened the door of the library. Passerat got up. The Baron said 'Good evening, Victor' and Passerat said 'Good evening.' Whereupon, being unwanted, I respectfully withdrew. *Sic transit gloria mundi.*"

"They will be sitting down having a drink," says Pablo who has cleaned himself up and is now regarding his hair from a distance in the oval looking-glass.

This way and that he turns his head, with its hair shiny-black.

"Didn't he ask for more ice?" says Eleanor. "They never have enough ice."

"They have plenty of ice in the drinks cupboard. I filled the ice-box, myself, and put more on refrigeration this afternoon when you were all busy with your telephoning and personal arrangements," Lister says. "They have ice. All they need now is the Baroness."

"Oh, she'll come, don't worry," says Clovis, stacking his papers neatly.

"I wish she'd hurry," says Heloise, as she slumps in a puffy cretonned armchair. "I want to eat my dinner in peace."

Hadrian has prepared a tray on which he has placed a dish of scrambled eggs, a plate of thin toasted buttered bread, a large cup and saucer and a silver thermos-container of some beverage. Eleanor, with vague movements, leaves her table-setting to place on the tray a knife, a fork and a spoon; then she covers the toast and the eggs with silver plate-covers.

"What are you doing?" says Hadrian, grabbing the knife and fork off the tray. "What's come over you?"

"Oh, I forgot," says Eleanor. "I've been in a state all day." She replaces the knife and fork with one large spoon.

Lister goes to the house-telephone, lifts the receiver and presses a button. Presently the instrument wheezes. "Supper on its way up to him in the attic," says Lister. "Yours will follow later."

The instrument wheezes again.

"We'll keep you informed," says Lister. "All you have to do is stay there till we tell you not to." He hangs up. "Sister Barton is worried," he says. "Him in the attic is full of style this evening and likely to worsen as the night draws on. Another case of intuition."

Hadrian takes the tray in his hands and as he leaves the room he asks, "Shall I tell Sister Barton to call the doctor?"

"Leave it to Sister Barton," says Lister, gloomily, with his eyes on other thoughts. "Leave it to her."

Heloise says, "I can manage him in the attic myself, if it comes to that. I've always been good to him in the attic."

"You better get some sleep after you've had your supper, my girl," says Clovis. "You've got a big night ahead. The reporters will be here in the morning if not before."

"It might not take place till six-ish in the morning," says Heloise. "Once they start arguing it could drag on all night. I'm intuitive, as Mr. Lister says, and—"

"Only as regards your condition," says Lister. "Normally, you are not a bit intuitive. You're thick, normally. It's merely that in your condition the Id tends to predominate over the Ego."

"I have to be humoured," says Heloise, shutting her eyes. "Why can't I have some grapes?"

"Give her some grapes," says Pablo.

"Not before dinner," says Clovis.

"Clara!" says Theo the porter. "Clara!"

"It's only that I'm burning with desire to ask them what's going on up at the house tonight," she says.

"Come back here. Come right back, darling," he says, drawing her into the sitting-room where the fire glows and flares behind the fender. "Desire," he says.

"Theo!" she says.

"You and your nightmares," Theo says. He shuts the door of the sitting-room and sits beside her on the sofa, absentmindedly plucking her thigh while he stares at the dancing fire. "You and your dreams."

Clara says, "There's nothing in it for us. We were better off at the Ritz in Madrid."

"Now, now. We're doing better here. We're doing much better here. Lister is very generous. Lister is very, very generous." Theo picks up the poker and turns a coal on the fire, making it flare, while Clara swings her legs up on to the sofa. "Theo," she says, "did I tell you Hadrian came down here to borrow a couple of eggs?"

"And what else, Clara," says Theo. "What else?"

"Nothing," she says. "Just the eggs."

"I can't turn my back but he's down here," says Theo. "I'll report him to the Baron tomorrow morning." He goes to draw the window-curtains. "And Clovis," he says, "for not keeping an eye on him." Theo returns to the sofa.

Clara screams, "No, no. I've changed my mind," and pushes him away. She ties up her cord-trimmed dressing-gown.

"Not so much of it, Clara," says Theo. "All this yes-no. I could have the Baroness if I want. Any minute of the hour. Any hour of the day."

"Oh, it's you that makes me dream these terrible things, Theo," she says. "When you talk like that, on and on about the Baroness, with her grey hair. You should be ashamed."

"She's got grey hair all places," Theo says, "from all accounts."

"If I was a man," says Clara, "I'd be sick at the thought."

"Well, from all accounts, I'd sooner sleep with her than a dead policeman," says Theo.

"Hark, there's a car on the road. It must be her," says Clara. But Theo is not harking. She plucks at his elastic braces and says, "A disgrace that they didn't have an egg in the house for the idiot-boy's supper. Something must be happening up there. I've felt it all week, haven't you, Theo?"

Theo has no words, his breath being concentrated

by now on Clara alone. She says, "And there's the car drawing up, Theo—it's stopped at the gate. Theo, you'd better go."

He draws back from his wife for the split second which it takes him to say, "Shut up."

"I can hear the honking at the gate," she says in a loud voice. "Don't you hear her sounding the horn? All week in my dreams I've heard the honking at the gate." Theo grunts.

The car honks twice and Theo now puts on his coat and pulls himself together with the dignity of a man who does one thing at a time in due order. He goes to the hall, takes the keys from the table drawer and walks forth into the damp air to open the gate beyond which a modest cream coupé is honking still.

It pulls up at the porter's lodge after it has been admitted. The square-faced woman at the wheel is the only occupant. She lets down the window and says, cheerfully, "How are you, Theo?"

"Very well, thanks, Madam. Sorry to keep you waiting, Madam. There was a question of eggs for the poor gentleman in the attic, his supper."

She smiles charmingly from under her great fur hat.

"Everything goes wrong when I'm away, doesn't it? And how is Clara, is she enjoying this little house?"

"Oh yes, Madam, we're very happy in this job," says Theo. "We're settling in nicely."

"You'll get used to our ways, Theo."

"Well, Madam, we've had plenty of experience behind us, Clara and me. So we've shaken down here nicely." He shivers, standing in the cold night, bareheaded in his porter's uniform.

"Your *rapport* with the servants—is that all right?" gently enquires the Baroness.

Theo hesitates, then opens his mouth to speak. But the Baroness puts in, "Your relationship with them? You get on all right with them?"

"Oh yes, Madam. Perfectly, Madam. Thanks." He steps back a little pace, as if only too ready to withdraw quickly into the warm cottage.

The Baroness makes no move to put her thick-gloved hand on the wheel. She says, "I'm so very glad. Among servants of such mixed nationalities, it's very difficult sometimes to achieve harmony. Indeed, we're one of the few places in the country that has a decent-sized staff. I don't know what the Baron and I would do without you all."

Theo crosses his arms and clutches each opposite sleeve of his coat just below the shoulders, like an isolated body quivering in its own icy sphere. He says, "You'll be glad to get in the house tonight, Madam. Wind coming across the lake."

"You must be feeling the cold," she says, and starts up the car.

"Good night, Madam."

"Good night."

He backs into the porchway of the cottage, then quickly turns to push open the door. In the hall he lifts the house-telephone and waits for a few seconds, still shivering, till it comes alive. "The Baroness," he says, then. "Just arrived. Anybody else expected?"

The speaker from the kitchen at the big house says something briefly and clicks off. "What?" says Theo to the dead instrument. Then he hangs up, runs out of the front door and closes the big gates. He returns as rapidly to the warm sitting-room where Clara is lying dreamily on the sofa, one arm draped along its back and another drooping over the edge. "You waiting for the photographer?" says Theo.

"What was all that talk?" Clara says.

"Shivering out there. She was in her car, of course, didn't feel it. On and on. Asked after you. She says, are we happy here?"

Pablo has got into the little cream coupé and driven it away from the front of the house as soon as Lister has helped the Baroness out of it, taken her parcels, banged shut the car door, and followed her up the steps and into the hall.

"Here," she says, pulling off her big fur hat in front of the hall mirror. Lister takes it while she roughs up her curly grey hair. She slips off her tweed coat, picks up her handbag and says, "Where's everyone?"

"The Baron is in the library, Madam, with Mr. Passerat."

"Good," she says, and gives another hand to her hair. Then she pulls at her skirt, thick at the waist and hips, and says, "Tell Irene I'll be up to change in half-an-hour."

"Irene's off tonight, Madam."

"Heloise, is she here?"

"Yes, Madam."

"Still working? Is she fit and well?"

"Oh, she's all right, Madam. I'll tell her to go and prepare for you."

"Only if she's feeling up to it," says the Baroness. "I think the world of Heloise," she says, stumping heavily to the library door which she opens before Lister can reach it, pausing before she enters to turn to Lister while the voices within suddenly stop. "Lister," she says, standing in the doorway. "Theo and Clara—they have to go. I'm so very sorry but I need the little house for one of my cousins. We don't really need a porter. I leave it to you, Lister."

"Well, Madam, it's a delicate matter at the moment. They won't be expecting this."

"I know, I know. Arrange something to make it

easy, Lister. The Baron and I would be so grateful." Then she throws open the door somewhat dramatically and walks in, while the two men get up from the grey leather armchairs. Lister waits in the room, by the door.

"Nothing, thanks, Lister," says the Baron. "We have everything here for the moment." He waves towards the drinks cupboard in a preoccupied way. The Baroness flops into a sofa while Lister, about to leave the room, is halted by the Baron's afterthought —"Lister, if anyone calls, we aren't on any account to be disturbed." The Baron looks at the ormolu and blue enamelled clock, and then at his own wristwatch. "We don't want to be disturbed by anyone whomsoever." Lister moves his lips and head compliantly and leaves.

"They haunt the house," says Lister, "like insubstantial bodies, while still alive. I think we have a long wait in front of us." He takes his place at the head of the table. "He said on no account to disturb them. 'Not to be disturbed, Lister.' You should have seen the look on her face. My mind floats about, catching at phantoms, and I think of the look on her face. I am bound to ventilate this impression or I won't digest my supper."

"Not a bad woman," says Pablo.

"She likes to keep grace and favour in her own

hands," Lister says, "and leave disagreeable matters to others. 'The couple at the lodge has to go, Lister,' she said, 'I rely on you to tell them. I need the lodge for my cousins,' or was it 'my cousin'?—one, two, three, I don't know. The point is she wants the lodge for them."

"How many cousins can she possibly have?" says Eleanor, looking at the clean prongs of her fork, for some reason, before making them coincide with a morsel of veal. "And all the secretaries besides."

"Cousins uncountable, secretaries perhaps fewer," says Lister, "if only she had survived to enjoy them. As it is the lodge will probably be vacated anyhow. No need for me to speak to the poor silly couple."

"You never know," says Heloise.

"Listen!—I hear a noise," says Pablo.

"The shutters banging upstairs," says Hadrian.

"No, it's him in the attic, throwing his supper plates around," Heloise says.

"It wasn't plates, it was a banging," Pablo says. "There it goes. Listen."

"Eat on," says Clovis. "It's only the couple of ladies in the car again. They're getting impatient."

"Why don't they ring?" says Lister as he listens to the thumping on the back door.

"I disconnected the back door bell," Clovis says. "We need our meal in peace. Since I was goaded to do most of the cooking it's my say that goes. Nobody leaves the table before their supper's over."

"Suppose one of them in the library rings for us?" Eleanor says.

Lister reaches out for his wine-glass and sips from it. The banging at the door continues. Clovis says, "It's doubtful if they will call us, now. However, we must no longer respond, it would be out of the question. To put it squarely, as I say in my memoir, the eternal triangle has come full circle."

"They've as good as gone to Kingdom Come," says Lister. "However, it is I who decide whether or not we answer any summons, hypothetical or otherwise."

"It's Lister who decides," says his aunt Eleanor.

II

It is ten-thirty at night. Lister has changed his clothes and so has his young aunt Eleanor. They walk hand-in-hand up the swirling great staircase with its filigree of Regency wrought-iron banisters, imported in their time as were so many other appointments of the house. Lister flicks on the light and opens the folding doors of the Klopstocks' long drawing-room, allowing Eleanor to pass before him into the vastness with its curtains looped along the row of French windows. Outside is a balustrade and beyond that the night. The parquet glitters obliquely, not having been trodden on today. The blue and shrimp-pink of the carpet, the pinks and browns of the tapestried chairs, the little tables, the scrolled flat desk and the porcelain vases are spread around Lister and Eleanor, as they enter the room, like standing waiters on the arrival of the first guests at an official reception. A porcelain snow-white lamb, artfully woolly, sleeps peacefully on the mantelpiece where the Baron placed it eleven years ago when the house was built and his precious goods brought in. The Adam mantelpiece at one end of the room came through the Swiss customs along with the rest as did the twin mantelpiece in the ante-room at the other end. Eleanor, wearing a grey woollen dress and carrying a black bag, sits down gracefully on a wide, upholstered chair and leans her arms on a small table, toying with the pink-blond carnations she herself arranged freshly this morning.

She looks about thirty-four. Her nephew, Lister, well advanced into his mid-forties. He wears a dark business suit with a white shirt and a dull red tie. They could be anybody, and more conceivably could be the master and mistress of the house just returned at this time of night from a trip to a city—Paris or even Geneva—or just about to leave for an airport, a night flight. Eleanor's hair is short, curled and dull. Lister's gleams with dark life. Their faces are long and similar. Lister sits opposite Eleanor and looks at a part of the wall that is covered with miniature portraits. Many objects in this large room are on a miniature scale. There are no large pictures, such as would fit it. The Monet is one of the smaller scale, and so is the Goya. So too are a group of what appear to be family portraits, so that it seems as if the inclination towards the miniature is either a trait descending throughout a few generations to their present owner, or else these little portraits have been cleverly copied, more recently, from some more probable larger originals. Ornamental keys, enamelled snuff-boxes and bright coins stand by on the small tables.

Lister looks away from the wall, and straight at Eleanor. "My dear," he says.

She says, "I hear their voices."

"They are still alive," says Lister. "I'm sure of that. It hasn't happened yet."

"It's going to happen," she says.

"Oh, my dear, it's inevitable." He takes a cigarette from the long silver box and lights it with the table lighter. Then he raises a finger for silence, as if Eleanor had been making a noise, which she had not. "Listen!" he says. "They're arguing in high tone. Eleanor, you're right!"

Eleanor takes from her bag a long steel nail-file, gets up, goes to a corner of the carpet, raises it, kneels, then with the file dislodges a loose piece of parquet.

"Softly and swiftly, my love."

She looks up. "Don't be so smart. This isn't the

time to lark about." She bends to dislodge another, and moving backward a little, knee by knee, leans forward on her elbows and places her ear to the planks of dusty common wood beneath the parquet.

"Eleanor, it isn't worthy of you," he says. "You look like a parlour maid. A minute ago you didn't."

She listens hard, looking upward through space to the high ceiling as if in a trance. Every little while a wave of indistinct voices from below reaches the drawing-room, one shrill, another shrill, then all together, excited. From a floor above, somebody bangs and the sound is repeated, with voices and a scuffle. Eleanor raises her head and says, exasperated, "With him in the attic barking again and banging, and you carrying on, it's impossible to hear properly what's being said below. Why didn't Sister Barton give him his injection?"

"I don't know," he says, leaning back with his cigarette. "I'm sure I advised her to. This parquet flooring once belonged to a foreign king. He had to flee his throne. He took the parquet of his palace with him, also the door-knobs. Royalty always do, when they have to leave. They take everything, like stage-companies who need their props. With royalty, of course, it all is largely a matter of stage production. And lighting. Royalty are very careful about their setting and their lighting. As is the Pope. The Baron resembled royalty and the Pope in that respect at least. Parquet flooring and door-handles. The Baron bought them all in a lot with the house when the old king passed away. They definitely came from the royal palace."

"All I heard from down there," says Eleanor, putting the oblongs of palace parquet back in place and rising, while she folds back the carpet over them, "was something like 'You said . . .' —'No you did not. I said . . .' —'No, you did say . . .' —'When in hell did I say . . .' That means they're going over it all, Lister. It could take all night."

"Heloise said it could be around six in the morning," Lister remarks as Eleanor stands flicking her skirt against the strange event that it has gathered fluff or dust. "Not," he says, "that I normally take any interest in Heloise's words. But she's in an interesting condition. They get good at guessing when they're in that state."

Eleanor is back in her chair again. Down at the back door there is a noise loud enough to reach this quiet room. A banging. A demand. At the same time, at the front door the bell shrills.

"I hope someone answers that door before the Baroness gets it in her head to go and answer it herself," says Eleanor. "Any break in the meeting might distract them from the quarrel and sidetrack the climax, wouldn't you think?"

"The Baron said not to disturb," says Lister, "as if to say, nobody leaves the room till we've had a clarification, let the tension mount as it may. And that's final. She'll never leave the library."

"Well, they must be getting hungry. They've had nothing to eat."

"Let them eat cake," says Lister, and he adds,

> "Think, in this battered Caravanserai
> Whose doorways are alternate
> Night and Day,
> How Sultan after Sultan with his Pomp
> Abode his Hour or two, and went
> his way."

Eleanor says, "It's true they've had some important visitors."

"The adjective 'battered,'" Lister says, looking round the quiet expanse of drawing-room, "I apply in the elastic sense. Also 'caravanserai' I use loosely. The house is more like a Swiss hotel, which you may be sure it will become. But endless caravans, so to speak, have most certainly come and gone here, they have come, they have stopped over, they have gone. I'm fairly to the point. It will make a fine hotel. Put different furniture into it, and you have a hotel."

"Lister," she says, "you're always so wonderful. There could never be anyone else in my life."

He says, rising to approach her, "Aunt to me

though you are, would you marry me outside the Book of Common Prayer?"

She says, "I have my scruples and I'm proud of them."

He says, "In France an aunt may marry a nephew."

"No, Lister, I stand by the Table of Kindred and Affinity. I don't want to get heated at this moment, on this night, Lister. You're starting me off. The press and the police are coming, and there are only sixty-four shopping days to Christmas."

"I was only suggesting," he says. "I'm only giving you a little thought for when all this is over."

"It's going too far. You have to keep your unreasonable demands within bounds. I'm old-fashioned beyond my years. One thought at a time is what I like."

"Let's go down," says Lister, "and see what the servants are up to."

As they come down the staircase voices rebound from the library. Lister and Eleanor continue silently and, turning into the servants' hall, Lister stops and looks at the library door. "What were they doing anyway, amongst us, on the crust of this tender earth?" he says. "What were they doing here?"

The other servants fall silent. "What are they doing here, anyway, in this world?"

Heloise, pink and white of skin, fresh from her

little sleep, says, "Doing their own thing."

"They haven't finished it yet," says Clovis. "I'm getting anxious. Listen to their voices."

"There must have been some good in them," Eleanor says. "They couldn't have been all bad."

"Oh, I agree. They did wrong well. And they were good for a purpose so long as they lasted," Lister says. "As paper cups are suitable for occasions, you use them and throw them away. Who brought that fur coat in here?" He points to a white mink coat draped over a chair.

"It looks a dream on me," Heloise says. "It doesn't meet at the front, but afterwards it will."

"You'd better put it back. Victor Passerat's been seen in it," Lister says. "The police will enquire."

Heloise takes away the coat and says, as she goes, "I'll get it in the end. Somehow I feel I'll get it in the end."

"She might well be right," Lister says. "Her foresight runs high at this moment. Who were those people banging at the back door and ringing at the front?"

"The girls in the car, demanding what's happened to their friend, Passerat," Hadrian says. "I told them that he was with the Baron and Baroness and they were not to be disturbed. They said they had an appointment. One of them's a masseuse that I haven't seen before."

"And the other?" says Lister.

"The other didn't say. I didn't ask."

"You did right," Lister says. "They don't come into the story."

Outside are the sounds of the lake-water lapping on the jetty and of the mountain-wind in the grandiose trees. The couple in the car are separated, one in the front, one in the back seat, each lolling under a rug. They seem to be sleeping but every now and then one of them moves, one of them speaks, and again their heads bend and the blankets move over their crouched uneasy shoulders. The lights from the house and from the distant drive touch on their movements.

They both start upright as another car, dark and large, pulls up. A lithe, leather-coated young man sprints out and approaches the couple. They are scrambling out of their car now.

"We can't get in the house," says the one from the front seat. "They won't open the door, even. We've been here over three hours, waiting for our friend."

"What friend? What do you want?" says the lithe young man, impatiently jangling a bunch of keys. "I'm the secretary, Mr. Samuel. Tell me what you want."

The other friend of Victor Passerat replies, "Victor Passerat. We're waiting for him. It's serious. He had an appointment with the Baroness and with the Baron, and—"

"Just a minute," says Mr. Samuel, looking closely at the second friend, "just a minute. You sound like a man."

"I am a man."

"All right. I thought you were a girl."

"That's only my clothes. My friend here's a woman. I'm Alex—she's a masseuse."

"My name's Anne," states the masseuse, stockily regarding Mr. Samuel's bunch of keys. "Do you have the keys to the house?"

"I certainly do," says Mr. Samuel.

"Well, we want to know what's going on," says the woman.

"We're worried, quite frankly," says her young friend.

Mr. Samuel places a gentle hand on the shoulders of each. "Don't you think," he says, "that it would be more advisable for you to go away and let nature take its course? Go away, quietly and without fuss; just go away and play the piano, or something. Take a soothing nightcap, both of you, and forget about Passerat."

From an upper room comes a sound like a human bark followed by an owl-screech.

Anne the masseuse adds a further cry to the night. "Open that door," she screams and, running to the back door, beats her heavy shoulder against it, banging with her fists as well.

Mr. Samuel winds his way to her with pleasant-mannered authority. "That was only the invalid," he says. "The nurse has probably bitten his finger again. You would do the same, I'm sure, if one of your patients attempted to place his hand over your mouth for some reason."

Anne's friend, Alex, calls out, "Come on back in the car, Anne. It might be dangerous."

Mr. Samuel is touching her elbow, urging her back to their small car. "There's nothing in it for you," he is saying. "Go home and forget it."

The masseuse is large but she appears to have very little moral resistance. She starts to cry, with huge baby-sobs, while her companion, Alex, his square bony face framed in a silk head-scarf and his eyes pleadingly laden with make-up under finely shaped eyebrows, puts out a bony hand to touch her face. "Come back in the car, Anne," he says, giving Mr. Samuel a look of hurt umbrage.

Anne turns on Mr. Samuel. "Who made you the secretary?" she says. "Victor Passerat has been secretary since June."

"Please," says Mr. Samuel. "I didn't say he wasn't secretary. I only say I'm the secretary in residence. There are I don't know how many secretaries. Victor is only one of the many and it's only just unfortunate that this appointment between him and the Baron Klopstocks should keep you hanging around outside the house on a cold night. Just go home. Put on a record."

"Is everything going to be all right?" Anne says. Alex has got into the car, waiting for her. Anne gets in and puts her hands on the wheel without certainty. She looks at Alex as if for guidance. Meanwhile Mr. Samuel has flicked himself in a graceful and preoccupied way to the back door of the house and now selects a key.

The couple in the car stare after him and he gives them one more glance; he lets himself in and quietly closes the door upon them. They drive off, then, up the long avenue, round the winding drive, past the lawns which in summer lie luminously green and spread on the one hand towards the swimming-pool in its very blue basin, and on the other towards the lily-pond, the animal-shaped yews, the fountains and the sunken rose garden. Behind them, and beyond the darkness, twinkles the back of the house—a few slits of light peppering its whole length—and behind that again, in the further darkness, the sloping terraces leading to the Lake of Geneva where the boats are moored and the water stretches across to the mountain shore. The little dark green car, leaving it all behind, reaches the lodge. Anne sounds the horn. Theo, wrapped up, now, in a heavy coat, stands evidently forewarned; he unlocks the gate and swings it wide.

When they have reached the main road and are off, he goes indoors; there he writes down the number of their car on a scribbling block which he has set out ready in the hall.

His wife stands by in her cord-trimmed dressing-gown. "Why are you doing that?" she says.

"I don't know, Clara. But seeing I've been told to expect an all-night spell of duty without any relief-man, I've been taking a note of all numbers. I don't know, Clara, I really don't know why." He tears off the sheet and crumples it, tossing it on the sitting-room fire.

"What's wrong with the relief-men tonight?" Clara says. "Where's Conrad, where's Bernard, where's Jean-Albert, where's Stephen? Why don't they send Pablo, what's he doing with them up there at the house? My sleep is terrible, how can I sleep?"

"I'm a simple man," says Theo, "and your dreams give me the jitters, but setting all that aside I smell a crisis. The Baroness hasn't been playing the game, and that's about it. Why did she let herself go to rack and ruin? They say she was a fine-looking woman a year ago. Lovely specimen."

"She used to keep her hair frosted or blond-streaked," Clara whispers. "She shouldn't have let go her shape. Why did she suddenly start to go natural?

She must have started to be sincere with someone."

"Don't be frightened, Clara. Don't be afraid."

"It's true what I say, Theo. She changed all of a sudden. I showed you her in the magazines in her ski-outfit. Wasn't she magnificent?"

"Go to bed, Clara. I say, go up to bed, dear."

"Can't I have the wireless on for company?"

"All right. Keep it low. We aren't supposed to be here to enjoy ourselves, you know."

Theo steps forth from his doorway as another car approaches the gate, flicking its large headlights.

The chauffeur puts his head out while Theo opens the gate, but Theo speaks first, apparently recognising the occupant of the back seat.

"His Excellency, Prince Eugene," Theo says, respectfully.

The chauffeur's mouth smiles a little, his eyes drooping, perhaps with boredom, perhaps with tiredness.

"I'm pretty sure they're not at home. Were they expecting his Excellency?" Theo says.

"Yes," says the visitor from the depths of the back seat.

"I'll just call the house," says Theo and returns to the lodge.

"Drive on," says Prince Eugene to his driver. "Don't wait for him and all that rot. I said to Klopstock I'd look in after dinner and I'm looking in after dinner. He should have told his porter to expect me." As he speaks, the car is already off on its meander towards the house.

Lister is waiting at the door. He runs down the steps towards the big car as the driver gets out to open the door for the Prince.

"The Baron and Baroness are not at home," Lister says.

Prince Eugene has got out and looks at Lister. "Who are you?" he says.

"Excuse me, your Excellency, that I'm in my off-duty clothes," Lister says. "I'm Lister, the butler."

"You look like a Secretary of State."

"Thank you, sir," says Lister.

"It isn't a compliment," says the Prince. "What do you mean, they're not at home? I saw the Baron this morning and he asked me to drop in after dinner. They're expecting me." He mounts the steps, Lister following him, and enters the house.

In the hall he nods towards the library door from where the sound of voices comes. "Go and tell them I'm here." He starts to unbutton his coat.

"Your Excellency, I have orders that they are not to be disturbed." Lister edges round so that his back is turned to the library door, as if protecting it. He adds, "The door is locked from the inside."

"What's going on?"

"A meeting, sir, with one of the secretaries. It has

already lasted some hours and is likely to continue far into the night."

The Prince, plump, with pale cheeks, refrains from taking off his coat as he says, "Whose secretary is it, his or hers?"

"The gentleman in question is the one who's been secretary to both, sir, for the past five months, nearly."

"Almighty God, I'd better get out of here!" says Prince Eugene.

"I would do that, sir," Lister says, leading the way to the front door.

"The Baron seemed all right this morning," says the Prince on the threshold. "He'd just got back from Paris."

"I imagine there have been telephone conversations throughout the afternoon, sir."

"He didn't seem to be expecting any trouble."

"None of them did, your Excellency. They were not prepared for it. They have placed themselves, unfortunately, within the realm of predestination."

"You talk like a Secretary of State to the Vatican."

"Thank you, sir."

"It isn't a compliment." The Prince, buttoning up his coat, passes out into the night air through the door which Lister is holding open for him. Before descending the steps to his car, he says, "Lister, do you expect something to happen?"

"We do, sir. The domestic staff is prepared."

"Lister, in case of investigations no need, you understand, to mention my visit tonight. It is quite a casual neighbourly visit. Not relevant."

"Of course, your Excellency."

"By the way, I'm not an Excellency, I'm a Highness."

"Your Highness."

"A domestic staff as large and efficient as yourselves is hard to come by. Quite exceptional in Switzerland. How did the Baron do it?"

"Money," says Lister.

The voices, indistinguishable but excited, wave over to them from the library.

"I need a butler," says his Highness. He takes out a card and gives it to Lister. Jerking his head towards the library door, he says, "When it's all over, if you need a place, come to me. I would be glad of some of the other servants, too."

"I doubt if we shall be looking for further employment, sir, but I thank you deeply for your offer." Lister puts the card in a note-case which he has brought out of his vest pocket.

"And his cook? That excellent chef? Will he be free?"

"He, too, has his plans, your Excellency."

"There will of course be a scandal. He must have paid you all very well for your services."

"For our silence, sir."

Upstairs a voice growls and the shutters bang.

"That's him in the attic," says Prince Eugene.

"A sad case, sir."

"He inherits everything."

"How, sir? He's a connection of the Baroness through her first marriage. A cousin of the first husband. I think the Baron could hardly bequeath a vast estate to him, poor thing in the attic. The Baron is succeeded by a brother in Brazil."

"The one in Brazil is the youngest. The one in the attic is next in line—no relation to her at all."

"That," says Lister, "I did not know."

"Few people know it. Don't tell anyone I said so. Klopstock would kill me. Would have killed me."

"Well, it makes no difference to us, sir, who gets the fortune. Our fortunes lie in other directions."

"A great pity. I would have taken on the cook. An excellent cook. What's his name?"

"Clovis, sir."

"Oh, yes, Clovis."

"But he will be giving up his profession, I dare say."

"A waste of talent." The Prince gets into his car and is driven away from the scene.

Mr. Samuel has taken off his leather coat and is sitting in the large pantry office which gives off from the servants' hall, looking through a file of papers. He leans back in his chair, dressed in a black turtle-necked sweater and black corduroy trousers. The door is open behind him and the large window in front of him is black and shiny with blurs of light from the courtyard, like a faulty television screen. A car draws up to the back door. Mr. Samuel says over his shoulder to the servants in the room beyond, "Here's Mr. McGuire, let him in."

"He has the keys," says Heloise.

"Show a little courtesy," says Mr. Samuel.

"I hear Lister coming," says Eleanor.

Mr. Samuel then gets up and comes into the servants' sitting-room. From the passage leading to the front of the house comes Lister, while from the back door a key is successfully playing with the lock.

Lister stops to listen. "Who is this?"

"Mr. McGuire," says Mr. Samuel. "I asked him to come and join us. I might need a hand with the data. I hope that's all right."

"You should have mentioned it to me first," says Lister. "You should have phoned me, Mr. Samuel. However, I have no objection. As it happens I need Mr. McGuire's services."

A man now appears from the back door. He seems slightly older than Mr. Samuel, with a weathered and freckled face. "How's everything? How's everybody?" he says.

"Good evening, Mr. McGuire," says Lister.

"Make yourself at home," says Clovis.

"Good evening, thanks. I'm a bit hungry," says Mr. McGuire.

"Secretaries get their own meals," says Clovis.

"I've come flat out direct from Paris."

"Heat him up something, Clovis," Lister says.

"Leave it to me," says Eleanor, rising from her chair with ostentatious meekness.

"Mr. Samuel, Mr. McGuire," says Lister, "are you here for a limited time, or do you intend to wait?"

Mr. McGuire says, "I'd like to see the Baron, actually."

"Out of the question," says Mr. Samuel.

"Not to be disturbed," says Lister.

"Then what have I come all this way for?" says Mr. McGuire, pulling off his sheepskin coat in a resigned way.

"To hold Mr. Samuel's hand," says Pablo.

"I'll see the Baron in the morning. I have to talk to him," says Mr. McGuire.

"Too late," says Lister. "The Baron is no more."

"I can hear his voice. What d'you mean?"

"Let us not strain after vulgar chronology," says Lister. "I have work for you."

"There's veal stew," Eleanor calls out from the kitchen.

"Blanquette," says Clovis, "de veau." He puts a

hand to his head and closes his eyes as one tormented by a long and fruitless effort to instruct.

"Do you have a cigarette handy?" says Heloise.

"There's a lot of noise," says Mr. McGuire, jerking his head to indicate the front part of the house. "It fairly penetrates. Who's the company tonight?"

"Hadrian," says Lister, taking a chair, "give a hand to Eleanor. Tell her I'd be obliged for a cup of coffee."

"When I was a boy of fourteen," says Lister, "I decided to leave England."

Mr. McGuire reaches down and stops the tape-recorder. "Start again," he says. "Make it more colloquial, Lister. Don't say 'a boy of fourteen,' say 'a boy, fourteen,' like that, Lister."

They sit alone in Lister's large bedroom. They each occupy an armchair of deep, olive-green soft leather which, ageless and unworn, seems almost certainly to have come from another part of the house, probably the library, in the course of some complete refurnishing. A thick grey carpet covers the whole floor. Lister's bed is narrow but spectacular with a well-preserved bushy bear-like fur cover which he might have acquired independently or which might have once covered the knees of an earlier Klopstock while crossing a winter landscape by car, and which, anyway, looks as if importance is attached to it; indeed, it is certain that everything in the room, including Mr. McGuire, is there by the approval of Lister only.

Between the two men, on the floor, is a heavily built tape-recorder in an open case with a handle. It is attached by a long snaky cord to an electric plug beside the bed. The two magnetic bobbins of the 18-centimetre size have come to a standstill at Mr. McGuire's touch of the stop-switch; the bobbins not being entirely equal in their content of tape it can be assessed that half-an-hour of something has already been recorded at some previous time.

Lister says, "Style can be left to the journalists, Mr. McGuire. This is only a preliminary press hand-out. The inside story is something else—it's an exclusive, and we've made our plans for the exclusive. All we need now is something for the general press to go on when they start to question us, you see."

"Take my advice, Lister," says Mr. McGuire, "and give it a conversational touch."

"Whose conversational touch—mine or the journalists'?"

"Theirs," says Mr. McGuire.

"Turn on the machine," says Lister.

Mr. McGuire does so, and the bobbins go spinning.

"When I was a boy, fourteen," says Lister, "I decided to leave England. There was a bit of trouble over me having to do with Eleanor under the grand piano, she being my aunt and only nine. Dating from that traumatic experience, Eleanor conceived an inverted avuncular fixation, which is to say that she followed me up when she turned fourteen and—"

"It isn't right," says Mr. McGuire, turning off the machine.

"It isn't true, but that's not to say it isn't right," Lister says. "Now, Mr. McGuire, my boy, we haven't got all night to waste. I want you to take a short statement of similar tone from Eleanor and one from Heloise. The others can take care of themselves. After that we have to pose for the photographs." Lister bends down, turns on the machine, and continues. "My father," he says, "was a valet in that house, a good position. It was Watham Grange, Leicestershire, under the grand piano. I worked in France. When Eleanor joined me I worked in a restaurant that was owned by a Greek in Amsterdam. Then we started in private families and now I've been butler with the Klopstocks here in Switzerland for over five years. But to sum up I really left England because of the climate—wet." Lister turns off the switch and stares at the tape-recorder.

Mr. McGuire says, "Won't they want something about the Klopstocks?"

Lister says, impatiently, "I am thinking." Presently

he turns on the recorder again, meanwhile glancing at his watch. "The death of the Baron and Baroness has been a very great shock to us all. It was the last thing we expected. We heard no shots, naturally, since our quarters are quite isolated from the residential domain. And of course, in these large houses, the wind does make a lot of noise. The shutters upstairs are somewhat loose and in fact we were to have them seen to tomorrow afternoon."

Mr. McGuire halts the machine. "I thought you were going to say that him in the attic makes so much noise that you mistook one of his fits for the shots being fired."

"I've changed my mind," Lister says.

"Why?" says Mr. McGuire.

Lister closes his eyes with impatience while Mr. McGuire switches on again. The bobbins whirl. "The Baron gave orders that they were not to be disturbed," Lister says.

"What's next?" says Mr. McGuire.

"Play it back, Mr. McGuire, please."

Mr. McGuire sets the reels in reverse, concentratedly stopping their motion a short distance from the beginning. "It would be about here," he says, "that your bit begins." He turns it on. The machine emits two long, dramatic sighs followed by a woman's voice—"I climbed Mount Atlas alone every year on

May Day and sacrificed a garland of bay leaves to Apollo. At last, one year he descended from his fiery chariot—"

McGuire has turned off, and has manipulated the machine to run further forward silently.

"That must be the last of your Klopstock soundtracks," Lister says.

"Yes, it is the last."

"You should have used fresh reels for us. We don't want to be mixed up with what Apollo did."

"I'll remove that bit of the tape before we start making copies. Leave it to me," says Mr. McGuire, getting up to unplug the machine.

"What is to emerge must emerge," says Lister, standing, watching, while Mr. McGuire packs the wire into place and fastens the lid on the tape-recorder. He lifts it and follows Lister out of the room. "It's a heavy machine," he says, "to carry from place to place."

They descend the stairs to the first landing of the servants' wing. Here, Lister leads the way to the grand staircase, followed after a little hesitation by Mr. McGuire who had first seemed inclined to continue down the back stairs.

"I hear no voices," Lister says as he descends, looking down the well of the great staircase to the black and white paving below. "The books are silent."

They have reached the ground floor. Mr. McGuire

stands with his heavy load while Lister approaches the library door. He waits, turns the handle, pressing gently; the door does not give.

"Locked," says Lister, turning away, "and silent. Let's proceed," he says, leading the way to the servants' quarters. "There remain a good many things to be accomplished and still more chaos effectively to organise."

"It must have happened quick. I wonder if they felt anything?" says Heloise. "Maybe they still feel something. One of them could linger."

Lister says, "I can't forbear to ask, does a flame feel pain?"

"Lister and young Pablo," says Mr. Samuel who is moving round the servants' room with his camera, "stand closer together. Lister, put your hand on the chair."

Lister puts his hand on Pablo's shoulder.

"Why are you doing that? It doesn't look good," says Mr. Samuel.

"Leave it to Lister," says Eleanor at the same time that Lister says, "I'm consoling him."

"Then Pablo must look inconsolable," says Mr. Samuel. "It's a good idea in itself."

"Look inconsolable, Pablo," says Lister. "Think of

some disconsolate idea such as your being in Victor Passerat's shoes."

The camera clicks quietly, like a well-reared machine. Mr. Samuel moves a few steps then clicks from another angle. He then moves a lamp and says, "Look this way," pointing a finger to a place in the air.

"Pablo smiled the second time," says Eleanor. "You want to be careful."

"Mr. Samuel knows that the negatives are mine," Lister says, "don't you, Mr. Samuel."

"Yes," says Mr. Samuel.

"Where is that wreath?" Lister says. "Where's our floral tribute?"

"On the floor in my room," says Heloise.

"Go and fetch it."

"I'm too tired."

"I'll go," says Hadrian, going. As he opens the door a long howl comes from above.

"Sister Barton failed to give him his injection tonight," says Lister, "and I wonder why."

"Sister Barton is upset. She didn't touch her supper," says Clovis.

"She's suffering from fear, quite a thrilling emotion," says Lister. "People love it."

"I sent up cold chicken breast and lettuce cut into shreds the Swiss way, which she imagines in her inexperienced little heart to be the right way," Clovis murmurs. He is standing with one hand on the belt that encircles his narrow hips. Several gold medallions hang from chains on his chest. Mr. Samuel's camera trains upon him, as he seems to expect it to do. He lowers his lids. "Good," says Mr. Samuel, moving round to Heloise.

"Head and shoulders only," says Lister at the same time as he answers a buzz on the house-telephone. "Him?" says Lister into the telephone. "Why?" The answer, fairly prolonged and intelligible apparently to Lister, is otherwise that of a bronchial and aged raven, penetrating the room, until Lister says, "All right, all right," and hangs up. Then he turns and says, "We've got the Reverend on our hands. He's come on his motor-bike from Geneva. Sister Barton has summoned him to soothe her patient."

"I smell treason," says Eleanor.

"How do you mean?" Lister says. "She always has been an outsider, so treason isn't the word."

"Well, she's a bitch," says Heloise.

"Here he is," says Lister, as the sound of a motor approaches. "Pablo, open the door."

Pablo goes to the back door but the sound of the motor recedes round the house towards the front. "He's gone to the front door," Lister says. "I'd better go myself."

He passes Pablo, saying, "Front door, front door, leave it to me," and, crossing the black and white squares of the hall, admits the Reverend.

"Good evening, Lister. I thought you'd be in bed," says the white-haired Reverend who carries a woollen cap in his hand.

"No, Reverend," says Lister, "none of us is in bed."

"Oh well, I came to the front thinking you were in bed. The light's on in the library, I thought the Baron might let me in." He looks up the staircase. "He sounds quiet, now. Has he gone to sleep? Sister Barton called me urgently."

"Sister Barton did wrong to bring you out, Reverend, but I must say I'm relieved to see you, and it just occurs to me after all, she may have done right."

"Your riddles, Lister." The Reverend is tall, skinny and wavering. He takes off his thick sheepskin coat. He wears a clerical collar and dark grey suit. He is quite aged, seeming to give out a certain life-force which perhaps only derives from the frailty of his appearance combined with his clear ability to come out on a windy night on a motor-bicycle.

He nods towards the library door. "Is the Baron alone?—I know it's late but I'd like to pop in and have a word with him before going on upstairs. I've many times sat up later talking to the Baron." The Reverend is already at the library door, waiting for Lister merely to knock and announce him.

"They are a party of three," says Lister. "I have

orders from the Baron, I'm sorry, Reverend, that they are not to be disturbed. Not on any account."

The Reverend, happily breathing the centrally heated air of the hall, sighs and then cocks his head slightly with sudden intelligence, his eyes bird-like. "I don't hear anybody. Are you sure that he has company?"

"Quite sure," says Lister moving away, sideways, backwards, indicating decisively the pathway that the Reverend must take. "Come in with us, Reverend, and warm up. A hot drink. Whisky and water. Something warm. I would like to talk to you personally, Reverend, before you see Sister Barton."

"Where? Oh, yes." The Reverend's eyes are losing their previous thread of reasoning and lead him in the precise footsteps of Lister's polished shoes.

"Good evening, I have something here," the Reverend says to the assembled room, putting his hand in his pocket, as Lister leads him in. "Before I forget." He brings out a small press-cutting and puts it on a ledge of the television table, sitting down near it. He feels in his inside coat pocket and pulls out his spectacles.

"Good evening, Reverend," and, "Nice to see you, Reverend," say Heloise and Pablo respectively while Hadrian comes in bearing, platter-wise under an airy cloud of cellophane, a large round flower-arrangement that looks as if it began as a wreath of laurel-leaves and was filled in according to taste with various rings of colour—red roses, double daffodils, white lilies, an inner ring of orange roses, and finally, at the bull's eye, a tight bunch of violets.

The sight seems to recall something to the Reverend. He moves his long bones to the process of getting up and says, "He hasn't died has he?"

"The Reverend means him in the attic," says Heloise.

Eleanor says, "I'll put them under the shower and give them a slight spray. Keep them fresh."

Lister, while assisting the Reverend to relax back into the seat, says, "We're having our photographs taken, Reverend."

"Oh!" says the Reverend. "Oh, I see," and, plainly, he is practised at habituating himself swiftly and without fuss to newer and younger notions however odd or untimely. He seems to be considering this as he warms to the room. Mr. Samuel brings his camera round and clicks at the pensive head, the loose and helpless hands of the Reverend. "Good," says Lister, bringing an elegant silver-cupped glass of softly steaming whisky on a tray from the kitchen, and stirring it with a long spoon. "Do another," he says to Mr. Samuel, standing back meantime, withholding the glass from the Reverend who has begun to stretch out his hand to receive it. The camera clicks smoothly upon the gesture of benediction. Then the Reverend gets his hot toddy.

"Good evening—or rather it's good morning, isn't it, Reverend?" says Mr. McGuire who comes in from the pantry office with his heavy tape-machine. "This is a pleasure," says Mr. McGuire.

"Mr. McGuire—good evening. I was in bed and the phone rings. Sister Barton is asking for me. It's urgent, she says, he's screaming. So here I am. Now I don't hear a sound. Everyone's gone to sleep. What are the Klopstocks up to, there in the library?"

Mr. McGuire says, "I really don't know. They're not to be disturbed."

"The Klopstocks and Victor Passerat," says Heloise.

"Heloise, it is not relevant who the guest is," says Lister. "It might be anybody."

Pablo has returned with Eleanor from the bathroom quarters where they have left the funeral flowers. He sits on the arm of Heloise's chair. The Reverend looks at the couple and reaches out for the newspaper cutting. He puts on his glasses. "I brought this along," he says. And again looks at the couple. He looks at the scrap of paper and looks hard at Pablo. "I cut it out of the *Daily American* for the Baron to read. It is quite relevant to the practices that go on in this house, and now I'm here and I see the Baron is busy, it seems to me that I can read it to whom it may concern." He looks at Pablo.

"Let's have it," says Pablo, leaning nearer to Heloise. She strokes her belly which moves involuntarily from time to time. Lister, seated at the table, silently points to the tape-machine and looks at Mr. McGuire.

Mr. McGuire heaves the machine on to the table while Lister says, "I don't quite gather all this, Reverend. Would you mind explaining again?"

Mr. McGuire is plugging his wire into the wall.

The Reverend now looks over his glasses at the tape-recorder. "What's that?" he says.

"It's the new electronic food-blender," says Lister. "We're all computerised these days, Reverend. The personal touch is gone. We simply programme the meals."

"Yes, oh yes." The Reverend suddenly looks sleepy. His head droops with his eyelids, and his hands with the newspaper cutting held in them move jerkily a fragment lower.

"Reverend, you were explaining about the newspaper item," Lister says, drawing on a cigarette. "Naturally, we are all receptive to any precepts you may have to cast before us, real swine that we are, we have gone astray like sheep. Every one his own way, numbered among the goats. Normally—"

"Yes, sex," says the Reverend, wakeful again. He

looks at Pablo, then at Heloise, then back to the cutting.

Lister says, "Normally it isn't a topic that we discuss between these four walls."

"You have to be frank about it. No point concealing the facts," says the Reverend severely.

Lister raises a finger and the discs of the machine begin to spin.

The Reverend says, "I brought this for Cecil and Cathy Klopstock to see. I think it might have something in it to help them with their problems. I hope it will help you with yours, every one of you." Then he reads, " 'New anti-sex drug'—that's the headline. 'Edinburgh, Scotland—Medical science has come up with a drug that keeps sex offenders under control, a doctor has reported to the Royal Medico-Psychological Association. The head of Edinburgh trials of the German drug told association members of the case of the forty-year-old man who had sexually assaulted a number of girls. The man had a history of indecent exposure, homosexual activity and a need for sex daily. But, three weeks on the new drug, cyproterone acetate, damped down his urges, the expert said. Three other subjects were given the drug. All the men reported being happier.' And so on, and so on. —Well," says the Reverend.

Lister raises a finger and the machine stops. "You have given out an interesting statement, Reverend," says Lister. "It should be heard and seen by all as a comment on many things that have been going on under this roof."

"That's what I thought," says the Reverend gloomily, putting away the press-cutting in his pocket. "I'd better go home," he says, then.

"The wind has died down," says Hadrian.

"He should spend the night here," says Eleanor. "He can't go all the way back to Geneva on that bike."

"Quite frankly, I got out of bed," says the Reverend. "Go and tell Klopstock I'm here."

"They are not to be disturbed. I had strict orders."

"I hope they aren't carrying on in the library. In the library. What time is it?"

"Just past quarter to three," says Lister.

"I should be in bed. You should all be in bed. Why did you bring me all this way?"

Lister goes to the house-phone, lifts the receiver, and presses a button. He waits. He presses again, leaving his finger on it for some minutes. At last comes a windy answer.

"Sister Barton," says Lister into the phone. "Why did you bring the Reverend all this way?"

The Reverend says immediately, "Oh, yes, of course, my poor boy upstairs," while Lister listens patiently.

The Reverend is creaking himself out of his chair.

Clovis, who has been sitting with his arms folded and his little mouth shut tight, jumps to help him.

Lister is heard to say, "There was no need," and replaces the phone.

Lister says to the Reverend, "Sister Barton says that him in the attic needed you, but now he's gone to sleep."

At that moment a long wail comes from the top of the house, winding its way down the well of the stairs, followed then by another, winding through all the banisters and seeping into the servants' hall. "She's woken him up," says Hadrian. "That's what she's done."

"It's deliberate," says Eleanor. "She wants to bother the Reverend, that's all."

"I wonder why?" says Clovis. "What's her trend?"

"Take me up," says the Reverend.

Heloise has gone to bed. She is propped up with pillows, drinking tea. At the foot of her bed, sitting on either side, are Pablo the handyman and Hadrian the assistant cook, both of them as absolutely young as Heloise.

"I really could sleep," she says. "I really feel like another nap."

"No," says Pablo. "Lister wants us all to be suffering from shock when the police arrive. Lack of sleep has the same effect, Lister says."

"I could act a state of shock at any time, and besides there's my condition." She yawns, balancing her cup of tea in her left hand while covering her mouth with her right. "Lister's wonderful," she says.

"Terrific," says Hadrian.

"Marvellous," says Pablo. "I never saw such a sense of timing."

From the floor above comes the noise of a sharp clap, followed by another and another.

"It sounds like guns going off," says Heloise.

"Well it isn't," says Pablo. "It's shutters. The wind must be rising again. I loosed those shutters really good, didn't I?"

"Let's put on a record," says Hadrian. He slides off the bed and goes to the gramophone to choose a record, first turning them this way and that, his sharp eyesight quickly discerning the details printed on either side of the disc, even though that part of the room is dim, the only light being that by Heloise's bed.

From above, the shutters make further reports, followed by a more subdued clatter from a window below. Hadrian puts on a record and sets it going. The noise fills the room for an instant until Hadrian turns down the volume.

Then, while Heloise lights a cigarette, the two boys dance to the rock music. Heloise puts her teacup on the table by her bed. She takes a comb from a fringed satchel which is lying on the bed and a hand-mirror from her bedside table. She lays them on the bed while she loosens her hair which has been pulled back, pony-tail style. Then she holds up the glass and begins to comb, swinging her shoulder a little in time to the rock vibrations, her tongue tapping the beat against her teeth. The boys dance, facing each other and swinging, their feet moving always in the same small area of shiny pinewood flooring.

Heloise's room is furnished much like that of a young daughter of the house. Posters, slogans and pin-up photographs cover part of the walls. The furniture is low-built with straight lines, and upholstered with dark red, black and yellow stuff. A white woolly rug lies askew before a desk piled with coloured magazines and crayons and some boxes of various medicines. The boys' feet just miss the rug as they continue to dance.

Heloise says, "She didn't drink much, I'll say that for her." She stubs out her cigarette.

Pablo stops dancing. He says, "You're thinking thoughts, Heloise."

Hadrian, who continues dancing by himself, says, "Heloise, relate."

"What do you mean, I don't relate?" she says.

"When you relate you don't ask what you mean. There's such a thing as a trend."

"Who do you think you are, you—Chairman Mao?"

Pablo starts dancing again. The record ends. He turns it over and puts on the other side.

"Clovis is all right, too," Heloise says. "I'll miss Clovis."

Pablo says, "He could stay with us. Why shouldn't he stay with us?"

"Clovis can stay with us," says Hadrian.

"The Baroness was natural," says Heloise. "I'll say that. Why shouldn't she be photographed and filmed in the nude?"

Hadrian stops dancing. "You know what?" he says. "Sorry for Victor Passerat I am not. Neither alive nor dead."

"Nor me," says Heloise.

"He had a kind of something," Pablo says, jerking his arms as he rocks.

"I know," says Hadrian. "But it didn't correspond."

"Funny that it had to be him," says Heloise.

Pablo says, "It could have been one of the others."

Hadrian says, "But she decided on him. She got hooked on him."

"It was inevitable," says Heloise.

"It could have been someone else," Pablo says. "Anyone could have made his mistake."

"There's such a thing as a trend," Hadrian says. "If

he was hooked on the Baron he should have coordinated."

"Well he didn't coordinate," says Heloise, putting her looking-glass back on the table, then lighting a cigarette.

They stop talking for a while. Heloise smokes her cigarette, languidly regarding the dance. When the music ends, the young men together silently choose another record and put it on. First Hadrian, then Pablo, start once more to dance, bobbing and swaying as if blown by a current which fuses out from the beat of the music.

After a while, Heloise says, "I like Mr. McGuire."

"The finest sound-track man in the business. He coordinates," says Hadrian.

"Very professional, though," says Pablo. "That kind of puts a division, doesn't it?"

"Mr. McGuire and Mr. Samuel," says Hadrian, "are in a class by themselves. You can't judge against them just because they made a success. They're a great team."

"They went to prison for it," Hadrian says.

"Is that true?" Pablo says, and simultaneously Heloise says, "Did they? When was that?"

"Yes, when they started the business six, seven years ago. Mr. Samuel told me a lot about it," Hadrian says, stopping his long spell of dancing without any sign of having spent energy. "Mr. Samuel told me," he says, "that they were doing it for small money. If you do a thing for peanuts you get caught for a crime. You have to do it privately for big money like everything else."

Pablo stops dancing and sits on the bed.

"How did they do it before?" he says.

"It was the same technique. Mr. Samuel did the photography and Mr. McGuire did the sound-track. They put code ads in the papers. They got a lot of responses."

"A lovely technique, they have," Heloise says. "I must say I liked it when they did me with Irene and Lister. Mr. McGuire kept saying, 'Speak out your fantasies,' like that. I didn't know what the hell to say, I thought he meant a fairy story, so I started with Little Red Riding Hood, and Mr. McGuire said 'That's great, Heloise! You're great!' So I went on with Little Red Riding Hood and Lister and Irene changed sides. They joined in with Red Hiding Hood. Lister was terrific as the grandmother when he ate me up. You can see in the film that I had a good time. Then Irene got eaten up by Lister's understudy. Mr. Samuel is an artist, I'll say that, his perspectives coalesce."

Hadrian says, "Eleanor always does her Princess bit. You can't get her to do anything else."

"Too old to change," Pablo says, "but she does it good. I like the Princess and the Pea where she can't sleep on her bed. You should always do your own thing in a simulation. It all works in. The Baroness shows up good doing the nun in the Congo with Eleanor doing the Princess bit. Puss in Boots is a big bore."

"I can do the nun in the Congo," says Heloise.

"So can I," says Pablo. "I like it."

"Goldilocks and the Three Bears is best," says Heloise. "They got the idea of fairy stories from me. It was my idea, or anyway, it just came to me."

"Are your health and security cards stamped up to date?" Pablo says.

"I don't think so," says Hadrian.

"Mine aren't," says Heloise. "I meant to remind the Baroness."

"Lister would have seen to it if it had mattered," Hadrian says. "Obviously, it doesn't matter." He takes up another record, looks at it, says, "The Far Fetchers. Not bad," and puts it on while Heloise says, "Anything goes for me." The boys are dancing now. Heloise says, "She went to finishing school in Lausanne and learnt to eat an orange with a little knife and fork without ever touching the orange."

"Who?" says Pablo.

"The Baroness."

The young men dance on.

"There must be fog coming up on the lake," says

Heloise. "I can see it in the room already. It gets through the double windows, even, doesn't it?"

Pablo begins to sing to the music. He sings: " 'Pablo, the Baroness wishes to see you.' —Knock, knock. 'Come in, Pablo.' —'Good-morning, Madam, anything I can do, Madam?' —'Pablo, the shutters upstairs, they bang so much. I think they must be loose.' —'Right away, Madam.' —'See you later, then.' —'See you at the party, Baroness.' "

"See you at the party," sings Hadrian.

"Don't make so much noise," says Heloise. "Lister's busy upstairs with the Reverend and Miss Barton."

"There's something going on up there," Hadrian says, stopping still as the music ends.

"Lister can adjust whatever it is. Lister never disparates, he symmetrises," Heloise says and lights a cigarette.

Pablo goes to the window and looks out at the fog. "Lister's got equibalance," he says, "and what's more, he pertains."

"Definitely," says Hadrian.

Mr. Samuel is sitting in a big chair looking through a bound typescript and Mr. McGuire is looking over his shoulder.

Clovis sits at a round table which is covered with blue velvet. His elbows are on the table and his chin rests gloomily on his hands.

"It's a winner," says Mr. Samuel. "Congratulations, Clovis."

"It has a great deal of scope," says Mr. McGuire.

Clovis raises then lowers his eyebrows. His look of gloom does not change, his elbows remain still.

"A first-rate movie script," says Mr. Samuel. "Some of the scenes are beyond belief. Only an authority on the subject could have pieced it together."

"The lines are terrific," says Mr. McGuire, running his fingers fondly over his tape-recorder which lies closed on the table. "You edited those tapes perfectly, Clovis."

Clovis remains mute.

Mr. Samuel says, "That's a good idea to open with, where you build up the Baroness like an identikit, when the police are looking for the motive and they put an eye here and a nose there. Very visual, Clovis."

"I'm waiting to hear," Clovis says. "We should have heard. Yesterday was the deadline."

"We'll hear," says Mr. Samuel. "Don't worry. The motion-picture industry is a very funny thing."

"The serialisation's come through," says Clovis, moving his right elbow from his chin in order to tap his hand on a bulky file which lies on the table. "That contract's safe."

"The film's in our pocket," says Mr. McGuire. "Our only problem is the casting. You have to have everyone younger than they really are. If Hadrian plays Lister, Pablo could play Hadrian."

"It's just that I wonder if they'll give Pablo the part."

"They'll have to," says Mr. McGuire.

"Eleanor can play the Baroness. The same shots as I've got, she only needs to follow the original film and dialogue," says Mr. Samuel.

"I'm worried about Pablo," says Clovis.

"He's very photogenic," says Mr. Samuel.

They fall silent as Lister enters the room followed by the Reverend.

"Where is Eleanor?" says Lister.

"Not here," says Clovis.

"Give the Reverend a nice drink," says Lister, going over to the house-phone.

"No, I should be in bed," says the Reverend. "I have to get up in the morning to see about the wedding."

"I'm sorry, Reverend, but we shall probably have an urgent mission for you in this house tonight arising out of Sister Barton's request. You really must stay."

"You must stay, Reverend," says Mr. McGuire. "We'll make you comfortable."

Lister has lifted the receiver and has pressed a button. He stands waiting for a reply which does not come. He presses another button, speaking meanwhile over his shoulder to those in the room. "Sister Barton," he says, "has asked the Reverend to perform a marriage service. She wants to marry him in the attic, who apparently assents so far as one can gather." Having got no answer from the phone he presses another button and meanwhile says to the others, "I've managed to dissuade the Reverend from such an irregular action at the present moment."

"She's out of her mind," says Mr. Samuel. "Off her head," says Mr. McGuire. And now Lister has got an answer on the phone. "Eleanor," he says into the speaker, "any news? Any luck?"

The answer whistles briefly. From outside the house comes a clap of thunder. Lister says into the speaker, "Be thorough, my dear," and hangs up.

"A storm in the distance coming over," says Mr. McGuire.

Clovis brings a glass of hot whisky to the Reverend who is sitting dazedly on the sofa. The Reverend takes the drink, and places it on the table by his side, with his fingers playing gently on the glass. He begins to hum a hymn-tune, then he nods with sleep, opening his eyes suddenly when a crackle of thunder passes the house, and letting them drop again when the noise is past.

The house-telephone rings. Lister answers it and it hisses back through its wind-pipe.

"Irene?" Lister says. "Yes, of course let her in. Use

your common sense." He hangs up. "That porter," he says to all in the room, "is a humbug."

The house-phone rings again. Lister takes the instrument off the hook very slowly, says into the speaker, "Lister here," and trains his ear on the garrulous sirocco that forces its way down the narrow flue of the phone. Meanwhile a car draws up at the back. A window can be heard opening above and Heloise's voice calls "Hi, Irene" into the stormy night. Mr. Samuel, who is peering out of the window, turns back to the room and says, "Irene in the Mini-Morris."

The house-phone in Lister's hand gives a brief gusty sigh. Lister says, "Darling, did you find the files locked or unlocked?"

The phone crackles amok while a double crash of thunder beats the sky above the roof. A long wail comes from the top of the house and from another level upstairs comes an intermittent beat of music. The back door rattles, admits footsteps and clicks shut. Lister at the phone listens on.

"Then be careful," he says at last, "not to lock them again. Leave everything as you found it. Take the copies and put the papers back. And hurry, my love. There is no cause for alarm—

But at my back I always hear
Time's wingèd chariot hurrying near—"

A tall skinny chinless girl with bright black eyes has come into the servants' room meanwhile.

Lister puts down the phone and says to her,

"And yonder all before us lie
Deserts of vast eternity.—

Where have you been all night, Irene?"

"It was my evening off," says Irene, removing her leather, lambskin-lined driving gloves.

"Evening off," says Lister. "What kind of an hour is this to return to the Château Klopstock?"

"I got caught in the storm," she says. "Good evening, Reverend. What a pleasure!"

The Reverend opens his eyes, sits up, lets his eyes wander round the room, then, seeing his drink he takes it up and sips it.

"Too strong," he says. "I'd like a cup of tea before I go."

"Listen to the storm, Reverend. You can't go all that way back to Geneva on your motor-bike tonight," says Lister.

"Out of the question," says Irene.

The outside telephone rings, piercing the warm room.

Lister says to Clovis, "Answer it. If it's a cousin wanting to talk to the Baron Klopstocks they are not to be disturbed. Who else could it be at this hour except a cousin?"

Clovis is at the switchboard of the outside telephone, in the pantry office. The Geneva exchange is speaking audibly in French. Mr. Samuel and Mr. McGuire stand behind him.

Clovis responds, then putting his hand over the speaker he says to them, "It's for me, from the United States."

"It's no doubt about the film," Lister says. "They should have telephoned yesterday. But it's still yesterday over there. They always ring in the middle of the night from the United States of America. They think that because they are five hours back we also are five hours back. Irene, go up and fetch Heloise and the boys. Bring them down here, we have things to discuss."

Irene goes and Lister once more takes up the house-phone, presses a button and waits for the hum. "Eleanor, are you coming?" he says. The house-phone gives vent as before, while thunder smacks at the windows and Clovis can be heard from the pantry office chatting joyfully to the United States. Lister says at length into the house-phone speaker, "Good, it's just what we need. Bring it down, love, bring it down at once. Put back the originals, and leave unlocked what you found unlocked and locked what was locked."

Clovis has come to the room again, followed by Messrs. McGuire and Samuel. The Reverend sleeps. Clovis smiles. "It's all tied up," he says, "and Pablo's getting the part of Hadrian, too."

IV

"At a quarter past seven, while the sky whitens," says Lister, "we all, with the exception of Mr. Samuel and Mr. McGuire, shall go up to our rooms, change into our smart working-day uniforms, and at eight or thereabouts we blunder downstairs to call the police and interview the journalists who will already have arrived, or be arriving. Mr. Samuel and Mr. McGuire will be in bed, but in the course of the breaking open of the library door by the police, they too will float down the staircase, surprised, and wearing their bath-robes or something seemly. We will by then have put the Reverend to bed and he can sleep on through the fuss until, and if, wakened by the police. He in the attic and Sister Barton will be back in their quarters. They—"

"Why should they be out of their quarters during the night?" Heloise says.

"Let me prophesy," Lister says. "My forecasts are

only approximate, as are Heloise's intuitions."

"Let Lister speak," says Eleanor.

The storm has moved away from the vicinity and can be heard in the distance batting among the mountain-tops like African drums.

Clovis says, "We've got nothing to hide. We're innocent."

"Well, we are crimeless," Lister says. "To continue with the plans. Heloise, you are pregnant."

The house-telephone rings. Eleanor lifts it up and bends an ear to its bronchial story. Heloise laughs.

"All right, let them come inside the gates. But don't let them out again," Eleanor says, and puts down the phone. She says to Lister, "That's Victor Passerat's two friends. They are threatening to call the police if we won't produce Passerat."

"Here they come," says Hadrian, at the window, and presently a car bumps up the drive. Presently again, a banging at the back door.

"Let them in," says Lister. "Bring them in here."

"That's right," says Clovis. "Better straighten things out."

Mr. Samuel goes out to the back door and returns followed by Anne the masseuse and her friend, Alex. They stand staring at the assembled household. They look from Eleanor to the dozing Reverend, they look at laughing Heloise, at Pablo and at long-legged Irene and Lister.

"I understand you want to use the telephone," Lister says. He waves towards the pantry office. "Well there it is."

"We want Victor," says Anne.

"He is in the library with the Baron and the Baroness. They're not to be disturbed. Strict orders."

"I feel afraid for Victor," says Alex.

"Why not ring the police as you've suggested?" says Lister waving again towards the pantry office. "The telephone's in there. We are having a busy night waiting up for the Baron and the Baroness."

"I'd rather keep the police out of it," Anne says.

"Yes, I dare say. What sort of reward are you hoping for, large or small?"

"Victor's our friend. We know Cathy Klopstock, too," says Anne.

Heloise says, "Why don't you call the police and tell them you've got those tape-recordings and films ready in your car, so that Victor and the Baroness can do a deal with the Baron, and then clear out? —Threats of exposure."

Eleanor says, "Don't be crude and literal, Heloise. This has been a tiring night. I wish you had bought some decent carrots for my juice."

"You have to be frank with these types," Heloise says.

"They don't connect," says Pablo.

"Come on, let's go," says Anne to Alex, whose eyes brim with tears.

They follow Mr. Samuel to the back door and leave the house.

"Heloise," says Lister, "as I was saying, you're pregnant."

Mr. Samuel comes back into the room as Heloise gives out her laughter.

Mr. Samuel says, "They've locked the doors of the car. Evidently they're going on a trip round the grounds."

Mr. McGuire goes to the window in the dark pantry office. "They've gone round to the front of the house," he says.

"Let them prowl," says Lister. "About your condition, Heloise. There's a solution to your problem."

"It's no problem," says Heloise.

"You marry the Baron," says Lister, "and become the Baroness."

Pablo says, "He's gone to meet his Maker. He shoots the wife and secretary when they talk too fast. Then he shoots himself, according to the script. He sorts out the mix-up the only way he knows."

"Eleanor has found some new evidence," Lister says. "It was quite unforeseen, but one foresees the unforeseen. He in the attic is the Baron's younger brother. Heir to the title and under the terms of the Trust, most of the fortune."

"I thought he was related to her, not him," says Hadrian.

"He's a nephew or something, isn't he?" Clovis says. "If not, I have to amend the script."

"A younger brother of the Baron."

"He turns my milk," says Heloise.

"Mine too," says Lister. "But he's the heir."

"There's the young brother Rudolph in Brazil," says Mr. Samuel. "He was always thought to be the heir. All that money."

"The one in Brazil is younger than him in the attic," Eleanor says. "Him in the attic is next in line. He inherits. Sister Barton knew what she was doing when she sent for the Reverend tonight and offered to marry her patient out of pity."

The Reverend has opened his eyes on hearing himself referred to. He has sat up, rather refreshed from his nap.

"My poor boy in the attic," he says. "Sister Barton is a fine woman. I think it should be done."

"He in the attic has prior responsibilities," says Lister. "Does anyone know his Christian name?"

"I never heard it mentioned," says Heloise.

"Sister Barton calls him Tony," says the Reverend.

"His name," says Lister, "is Gustav Anthony Klopstock. It's on his birth certificate, his medical certificate exempting him from army service, and it's in their father's will."

"The Registers?" says the Reverend.

"He's also mentioned in a social register for 1949. That's the latest we have in the house. It occurred to me he must have died, but I was wrong. I admit we were in error," Lister says. "But fortunately we left room for error, and having discovered it in time, here we are. There is a vast difference between events that arise from and those that merely follow after each other. Those that arise are preferable. And Clovis amends his script."

"I wouldn't have married him for choice," says Heloise. "He doesn't cognate."

"You don't have to cognate with him," says Hadrian. "You only need get your marriage-lines in black and white."

"Reverend," says Lister, "do you recall that night last June when the Klopstocks were away and him in the attic got loose? Remember we called you in to catch him and calm him down?"

"Poor boy, I remember, of course," says the Reverend. "He didn't know what he was doing."

"He's not officially certified," says Eleanor. "The Baron and Baroness wouldn't hear of it."

"That's true," Lister says. "And I wish to draw the Reverend's attention to the result of that rampage last June." Lister indicates Heloise who smiles at her stomach.

"Good gracious me!" says the Reverend. "I wouldn't

have thought he had it in him."

"We must lose no time," says Lister getting up. "Prepare the drawing-room, Eleanor. It's past five o'clock. I'll go and give orders to Sister Barton."

"I would need a few days," says the Reverend firmly. "You can't marry people like this."

"It's a special case, Reverend. You can't refuse. In fact, you may not refuse. Look at poor Heloise, her condition."

The central posy of violets is missing from the funeral wreath which lies under the shower in the scullery bathroom being gently sprinkled to keep it fresh. Heloise in her bedroom holds the posy in her hands. Pablo stands by admiringly. "I've unpacked all my things again," he says.

"What a business," she says. "Nobody needed to pack their things, after all. All those trunks and suit-cases."

Hadrian appears at the door of her room holding the white mink coat lately left in the cloak-room by Victor Passerat. "Just right for the occasion," she says, putting it on.

"Lister says it has to go back in the cloak-room immediately after the ceremony," Hadrian says. "The police will want to know what coat he was wearing. Lister is keen that the police should see this coat. It speaks volumes, Lister says."

"It doesn't meet in the front," Heloise says.

"You look nice," Pablo says.

There is a knock at the door and Irene walks in.

"You really going to marry him?" she says.

"Sure," says Heloise. "Why not?"

"Then you'll need some music," Irene says. "How can you have a wedding without music?"

"Eleanor could play the grand piano," says Hadrian.

"No," says Heloise. "I like Eleanor but she's got a lovely touch on the piano. I can't stand that lovely touch."

"Mr. Samuel plays the piano and also the guitar," Pablo says. "Mr. Samuel energises."

"Bring down the gramophone," says Heloise. "That's better; because Mr. Samuel will be taking the photographs and Mr. McGuire has to do the sound-track. This thing's got to go on record. It's got to compass."

"It's still stormy," says Hadrian as a flash of lightning stands for a second in the square pane of the window. A clap of thunder follows it. "There must be trees felled in the park," he says.

"I shall arrange for them," says Heloise, "to be swept up some time tomorrow. Let's go down to the room. They're all waiting."

Upstairs there is a scuffle and a howl.

"Isn't it usual for the bridegroom to arrive first?" says Irene.

"It's all right if he's late on account of his health," says Pablo. "Let's go."

"Clara," says the porter, "your tea, dearest. It's nearly half-past five, and I'm early bringing it up. I've got the jitters, somehow. I've just got orders not to open the gate before eight, and after that let everyone in. 'Absolutely everyone.' Can you understand it? Why should everyone come at eight in the morning?"

"Oh, my dreams, Theo," she says, sitting up in bed and reaching for her frilly bed-jacket. She puts it on and takes her tea from Theo's waiting hand.

"He said, 'Let everyone in after eight o'clock, not before.' This job's beyond me, Clara. We have to move on."

"Oh, but I love this little house. It was always what I wanted. You know I think the Baroness got sentimental with one of the secretaries. I think she's going to run away with him."

"Those two strange ones who came in the green car asking for Victor Passerat all the time," Theo says. "They came back up here a few minutes ago. They didn't get to see Victor Passerat. Now they're anxious to go home but I've got orders not to let them out. The gates don't open till eight, then everyone, absolutely everyone, can come and go as they please."

"Where have they gone then, those two?"

"Back to the house to wait there."

"Do you know, Theo, the one that sat beside the driver doesn't look like a lady. Very hard face. Like a man."

"Don't dwell on it, Clara dearest."

The drawing-room is being re-arranged for the wedding. Irene and Eleanor bustle and give orders to Pablo and Hadrian who are moving chairs and tables. The Reverend wanders with a perplexed air from one end of the room to the other, carefully piloting himself around the busy workers, weaving in and out between the minute tables and small sofas, and puzzling his brow absentmindedly at the tiny portraits and litter of small ornaments.

"I really think," says the Reverend, pulling his press-cutting out of his pocket, "that Baron Klopstock should take this pill."

"Too far gone," says Hadrian, standing back to see if the table he has placed beside another squares off neatly. "He's past caring."

Clovis comes in with an embroidered tablecloth which he lays carefully across the two oblong tables which Hadrian has placed end-to-end. "It makes a very good altar," says Clovis. He snaps his fingers. "A large candelabrum from the dining-room!" he shouts. Irene skips out of the room, while Lister with Heloise on his arm appears in the doorway of the ante-room at the far end.

The Reverend puts his press-cutting back in his pocket.

Eleanor says, "We are to use the Book of Common Prayer appointed to be read in the Church of England."

The Reverend says, "I always marry according to the Evangelical Waldensian form, which is very free."

"Heloise," calls Eleanor, her voice rising on the last syllable, "what religion are you?"

"None," says Heloise. She lets go Lister's arm, comes in from the ante-room and relaxes into a comfortable chair.

"What religion were you brought up in?" says the Reverend.

"None," says Heloise.

"Where were you born?"

"Lyons," says Heloise, "but that was by chance."

"It should be Evangelical," says the Reverend.

"In this house it is the Book of Common Prayer," Eleanor says. "Do you want her to have that child out of wedlock? We haven't all night to spend arguing, Reverend. The father has assented but he might change his mind."

"Let me see the English book, then," says the Reverend. "I have it within my competence to make exceptions in a case like this. Perhaps I could simplify the English form. I don't read well in English, you know."

Eleanor points to a flat, leather-bound book lying ready beside the small porcelain statuettes on a wall-table. "That's it," she says. "It can't be simplified, it's impossible."

Lister advances into the room, stopping to twist a bowl of flowers to better taste. He says, "Eleanor, the bridegroom is C. of E., I think."

"No, they're Catholics."

"Oh well, he went to Winchester, an English school."

"No, he never went to school. He was always unable."

"He went for a week."

"It isn't enough."

"Eleanor," says Lister, "we can have any little irregularity put straight later."

"That's right," says Heloise. "This coat's heavy."

Irene comes in with a large branched candlestick in ornamental silver with long white candles set in its sockets. She places it on the covered table.

"Don't light the candles yet," says Eleanor, raising her eyes to the ceiling, from above which comes the sound of a scuffle and a howl. "Goodness knows what might happen. We don't want a fire."

"He's had his injection," Lister says.

"Well it hasn't taken yet," says Heloise.

"Come back into the little room and stand with me," Lister says to Heloise. "The bride should enter last and enter last she will."

The scuffle upstairs continues and is accompanied by a repeated banging.

"Is that the wind or is it him?" says Eleanor. "Is it the shutters?"

"It could be either," Pablo says, listening expertly.

"I'd better go and help," says robust Hadrian. He bounds out of the drawing-room and up the stairs.

Heloise has again joined Lister at the door between the ante-room and the drawing-room and from there he gives his final instructions. "Remove the Sèvres vases—take them away, just in case. Irene, your skirt's too short, this is a ceremony."

Heloise says, "Irene likes to show her legs. Why not?"

"They're all she's got," says Clovis.

"He's coming!" says Irene.

The wind now whistles round the house and the remote shutters bang as another latent storm wakes up. Footsteps descend heavily and the occasional howl that accompanies them becomes, as it approaches, more like a trumpet call.

Mr. Samuel now enters with his camera. Mr. McGuire follows with his tape-recorder which he places on a table in an angle of the room, unplugging a lamp to make way for the plug of his machine. He tests it out, then pulls up a chair and, folding his arms, waits.

As the footsteps and the trumpet-blast tumble their way down, Pablo puts a record on the gramophone with a pleased but unsmiling expression. It is a new rendering of "Greensleeves," played very fast even at the beginning, and plainly working up to something complex and speedy.

"Not so loud," says the Reverend, but his words cannot be heard at the door of the ante-room, where Pablo has settled the gramophone by the side of Heloise and Lister. "Play it more quietly," Lister says.

Pablo turns it down.

"It seems unsuitable but one has to go along with them," says the Reverend as Hadrian and Sister Barton edge into the drawing-room, supporting between them him from the attic. It is immediately noticeable that the patient's howls and trumpetings appear to be expressions of delight rather than pain, for he grins incessantly, his great eyes glittering with ecstatic gladness.

Lister, with Heloise on his arm, advances slowly to meet the bridegroom. "What a noise he's making," says Heloise.

"There must be at least eighty-two instruments in that band you've got for your wedding march,"

Lister says, "another can't be amiss." An instant of quick lightning at the windows followed by a grumble of thunder reinforces his argument.

The zestful cretin's eyes fall first on Irene. He neighs jubilantly through his large teeth and shakes his long white wavy hair. He wears a jump-suit of dark red velvet fastened from crotch to collar-bone with a zip-fastener. This zipper is secured at the neck by a tiny padlock which very likely has been taken, for the purpose, from one of the Baroness Klopstock's Hermès handbags. Beside him, holding him fast with one arm round his shoulders and with the other hand gripping his arm, is a young nurse whose youthfulness does not help. Hadrian, his eyebrows tentatively raised, holds the other arm.

"My boy," says the Reverend to him from the attic who now stands shaking off his keepers with his powerful shoulders.

The other servants stand back, and Hadrian joins them. Eleanor casts a glance behind her to the open door, and stands a little nearer to it.

"A vivacious husband," says Lister. "Miss Barton, try to hold him firm. It's an exciting moment in his life."

"It's a scandal," says young Sister Barton. "It's me he wants to marry."

At the moment he seems to prefer Irene, and, breaking loose, plunges upon her. Heloise says, "He doesn't level, you can't really construe with him."

He is lifted off Irene, who demands a cigarette, and he is then consigned, still wishfully carolling, to the strong arms of Hadrian and Pablo.

"Make it look like something," says Mr. Samuel, training his camera. Immediately they open their mouths in laughter to combine with his, and group themselves on either side of him so that their restraining arms are concealed, only Hadrian's arm of fellowship and Pablo's congratulatory hand in the bridegroom's being revealed. Mr. McGuire's bobbins whirl sportively while the scene lasts.

"Just hold him there," says Lister, "for a minute."

But now the captive has caught sight of the bride, tall, pink and plump, and indicates his welcome with a huge fanfare of delight, straining mightily towards her.

"Reverend," says Miss Barton, "this is not proper. He's had his injection and these girls are simply nullifying the effect. In his normal state he is very much attached to me."

"This bit of group-therapy," Lister tells her, "is precisely what he needs. Poor man, confined up there all the time with you!"

"I am perplexed," says the Reverend. "I have to know which one he wants to marry." He smiles at the prisoner and says, "My boy, which of the ladies is your preference, if any?"

The bridegroom gives a cunning heave, triumphantly dragging Pablo and Hadrian in the direction of Heloise who is now taking a light for a cigarette from Irene's. He also spares a glance of beatitude for Eleanor, but continues to make for Heloise with determination.

Lister says, "It's Heloise, obviously." The storm beats on the windows and detonates in the park. The music comes to an end, causing him from the attic to crow and romp a little, and to touch the padlock of his zip lovingly.

"He wants to take his clothes off," says Sister Barton. "Take care. He's been known to do it."

"Who is the father of your child?" says the Reverend desperately to Heloise.

"Well," says Heloise, taking a chair, "it isn't born yet. Four months and a bit to go. Pablo was busy helping the Baron every evening at the time and Hadrian was off-duty. Mr. Samuel and Mr. McGuire were in the Baron's team, too, following their respective professions. Then—"

"The Baron?" says the Reverend impatiently. "Don't tell me he's never attempted to exercise *droits de seigneur*, because Baron Klopstock was well known in his youth."

Lister says, "A pornophile, merely. Pornophilia does not make for fatherhood, Reverend. At least, in my experience, it doesn't. Now, if the Baroness could have been the father in the course of nature she might have been, but the Baron, no."

"Let me see," says the Reverend, looking round the room. "Who does that leave?"

"All the rest of them," says Heloise. "Let's have some music."

"Someone from outside," says the Reverend.

"Do you mean one of the guests at one of the banquets, Reverend?"

"No, one of their private affairs, perhaps."

"Heloise was strictly on duty at the time," says Lister. "Very busy. The secretaries were fully occupied and there were no visiting cousins. You saw for yourself how it was the month of June. You were a constant visitor at large."

"Then it rests between Clovis, the poor boy Klopstock here, and you, Lister," says the Reverend, ticking them off again on his fingers while mentally going through the roll-call.

Lister whispers in the Reverend's ear.

"Oh," says the Reverend. "Well it isn't Clovis. That leaves you and the poor boy."

"I am enamoured to the brim with Eleanor," says Lister, "and her prayer-book carry-on."

"Lister," says Eleanor.

"Eleanor," he says.

"It's got to be him in the attic," says Heloise. "I'm waiting."

"It could only be him or the Reverend," Lister says.

"Let us begin," says the Reverend. "Bring him over—carefully, carefully. He must stand here with the girl."

"The music," says Heloise.

"Sister Barton," says Pablo, "if you don't come and help I can't go and put on the wedding record for Heloise."

"It's atrocious," says Sister Barton, weeping but not helping. "To take him away from me now, after all I've done."

The Reverend looks for a moment at Sister Barton then looks away as if finding her unsavoury. "Have you got a Protestant Bible?" he says. "If not, we'll do without."

"The English Prayer Book," says Eleanor, but she cannot be heard above the noise of the storm and the ecstasy of the man from the attic, whom Clovis is now assisting Hadrian to hold. Standing beside Heloise the patient is apparently dumbstruck and gazes at her with only his grin. "Greensleeves" starts up again.

"It's getting late," says Lister.

"The Book of Common Prayer," says Eleanor.

"It's within my competence as a pastor to perform a legal marriage in this country according to my own simple formula," says the Reverend looking at his watch then at him from the attic, while pointing to

Heloise. "Gustav Anthony Klopstock, do you take this woman to be your wedded wife?" he says.

The bridegroom escapes, once more, to tumble upon Heloise.

"That means 'I do,'" says Pablo, helping, with the others, to rescue the bride.

"Nobody can now say he wasn't in his right mind at the time of the marriage," says Lister. "He knows perfectly well what he's doing."

"In my condition," says Heloise.

When the couple are set in place again the Reverend says to Heloise, "What is your father's name?"

"Klopstock," says Heloise.

"Klopstock?"

A howl of delight is emitted by the Klopstock from the attic.

"Kindred and Affinity!" shrieks Eleanor above the boisterous instrumentals of the storm, the music and the groom.

"It is a coincidence," Lister says, spreading his hands like a conductor of an orchestra pleading a *pianissimo*. "Her father is a humble Klopstock, a riveter. No connection with the House of Klopstock whose residence this is, where galaxies of generals, ambassadors, and their bespangled consorts mingle with cardinals and exiled Arabians by night when the Baron and Baroness are not privately engaged."

"Are you of age?" says the Reverend to Heloise.

"I'm twenty-two," she says, swinging a little to the rock-music as it speeds up, and shaking the white mink coat.

"She's twenty-three!" says Sister Barton, still tearful.

"Well you're a major," says the Reverend to Heloise. "Heloise Klopstock," he says, "will you take this man to be your wedded husband?"

"I will," says Heloise.

"They have no ring," says the Reverend looking round irritably.

Lister produces a ring immediately.

"He'll only put it in his mouth and swallow it," weeps Sister Barton.

"I shall place the ring on the bride's finger by proxy," says Lister, doing so.

"I hereby pronounce you man and wife," says the Reverend, placing his hands on the shoulders of Heloise and her new husband who, now overjoyed, once more leaps out of reach, this time gambolling to the far end of the room. Numerous precious vases crash to the floor.

Mr. McGuire hastens to protect his bobbins, while Mr. Samuel says, clicking his camera, "Marvellous! his laugh's very like a large-mouthed cry of elation such as any beauty queen might give at the moment of her election."

"I would never resemble him to that," says Heloise.

Her husband is sprightly and will not be caught. He rips the whole zip-fastener from the stuff of his suit and exultantly dances out of the garment. Then, capering lustily with carols and further damage to the furniture, he pulls the mink coat off his wife's back, drags her into a corner and falls on top of her.

Pablo rushes to intervene.

"Leave him be. He has every right," says Lister.

"He has no right at a wedding," says the Reverend. "It's not the thing to do."

Sister Barton sobs and the storm revels, while Heloise shoves with hard athleticism and finally escapes, fleeing to the safety of the sound- and film-track area. "Give me a comb," she says.

Clovis is blowing out the candles.

Mr. Samuel says, "This will need a lot of editing."

"In my condition," says Heloise, "and I've lost a shoe."

The bridegroom is being held by Sister Barton, Hadrian and Pablo, and is being clothed with the embroidered tablecloth by Eleanor.

"Bite his finger and keep him quiet," says Clovis to Sister Barton.

"He was only doing his thing," says Hadrian.

Lister says, "Kings and queens of olden days used to consummate in public. They had four-poster beds with curtains. The court had to stand by to see the curtains shake when Mary Queen of Scots married the Dauphin of France, compared to whom our friend from the attic, here, is an Einstein. And so, my dear Heloise, nobody can now contest the validity of your nuptials on the grounds that they haven't been consummated."

"They were not consummated," says Heloise. "Only almost."

"To the eye of the candid camera," says Lister, "the marriage was consummated. Isn't it so, Mr. Samuel?"

"Yes," says Mr. Samuel. But nobody is listening. Lister is offering a pen and two sheets of typewritten paper to the Reverend. "The marriage certificate," he says. "Will you sign your witness, Reverend? I have already signed. In duplicate."

The Reverend is looking round him as if wondering where he is.

"Sign?" he says. "Oh yes, of course, I'll put my name. And the happy couple has to sign, too." He beams at everyone, takes out his glasses, rests the piece of paper on Eleanor's flat prayer book and signs. "The bridegroom," he says, "then the bride."

"Bite his finger," says Clovis to Sister Barton, "or you're fired."

Tearfully, she takes the little finger of the trumpeting patient in her mouth and bites. He starts to giggle and, although she lets go, does not stop. Lister places the pen in the giggler's hand and, raising the paper and the hard book to a convenient level, moves the limp and helplessly amused hand over the space provided until the name is traced, Gustav A. Klopstock. "The Anthony would have taken too long," says Lister, very satisfied in his expression of face. "You never know when his milder spells will stop. Now, Heloise." Heloise takes the pen and writes her name above the typed address, in the space reserved for her. "We register this tomorrow," says Lister. "It's a quarter to seven. Time has flown. Sister Barton, Pablo will assist you. Give him a nice warm drink and an injection."

"I must go home to bed," says the Reverend. "Where did I leave my bike?" He looks around the very untidy drawing-room.

"In this storm," Lister says, "you can't ride back to Geneva, Reverend. We have a bed for you. We shall always have a bed for you, Reverend. Eleanor, show the Reverend to his room."

"Nice of you, very kind under the circumstances," says the Reverend. "I want to show a press-cutting to Cecil Klopstock. Where is he?"

"The Baron is not to be disturbed."

"Tell him I want to see him when he wakes up."

V

"Bear in mind," says Lister, "that when dealing with the rich, the journalists are mainly interested in backstairs chatter. The popular glossy magazines have replaced the servants' hall in modern society. Our position of privilege is unparalleled in history. The career of domestic service is the thing of the future. The private secretaries of the famous do well, too. Give me another cup of coffee, please Eleanor. It's almost time to go up and change."

They are seated round the large table where breakfast seems to be as rapidly begun as nearing its end. The storm has retreated from the near vicinity of the house, but continues to prowl on the lake and the mountain-sides. Every now and again there is a banging of fists, a shouted demand, on the back door. Nobody takes any notice.

"Are there any grapes in the house?" says Heloise.

"No, you had the last of them," says Clovis.

"Well, you're wrong," says Irene, "because I brought her a huge big bunch from Geneva. They're in the pantry. I got them from that boyfriend who's a steward on the first-class TWA.

"Irene, what a treasure the Klopstocks have lost in you by their death!" says Lister.

Irene looks modestly at her crumby plate.

Clovis yawns and leans his elbow on the table and his head on his hands. "I'm worn out," he says. "I'll be glad to get to bed." He gets up, goes into the pantry and returns with a tray on which are set a plate of large green grapes, a bowl of water in which to dip them and a tiny pair of scissors with which to snip them off their twigs. He places them before Heloise. "Long live the Baroness!" he says.

Heloise pats her stomach.

Mr. Samuel then goes to open the back door. He can be heard saying, "You'll have to wait. Victor Passerat's not available just yet."

"We've lost the keys of the car!" says the woman's voice.

"Well, look for them."

"The ground's all wet. We're soaked through. Can't we come in and telephone to a garage, or something?"

"Sorry, strangers aren't permitted."

"What can we do? We can't get in the car, and we

can't get out of the gate. The porter won't open it for us."

"Take a stroll in the grounds," advises Mr. Samuel.

"It's wet. We'll get caught in another downpour. This is a terrible place."

"You should always," says Mr. Samuel, "avoid terrible places."

Returning to the servants' dining-room he says, "Amateurs. Where's my camera? It's just possible I could get a few shots of them to fit in an educational film I've got going. The young have to be taught about the average aberrant in the street."

He takes his camera to the window and focuses.

Lister, dressed smartly for the day's work, stands at the open front door like a gloomy shopkeeper looking at the dark, rumbling sky as Theo comes up the drive on his bicycle. Theo makes a questioning sign, pointing round to the back of the house. "No, come here," says Lister.

Theo tremorously parks his bicycle against the dripping hedge and walks the rest of the way.

"I called for you, Theo, because there is something strange to report," Lister says. "Come right in."

The others are coming downstairs, with sleeplessness in their movements and on their faces. The servants are dressed in their morning overalls. Behind them come Mr. Samuel in a knee-length blue bathrobe and Mr. McGuire in a black and white striped dressing-gown.

"What's going on?" says Mr. Samuel.

Theo says, "There's something peculiar been going on all night."

"Do you like the job, Theo?" says Lister.

"Yes, Lister," he says.

"Well, you can keep it. Only remember that nothing peculiar has been going on, as indeed it hasn't. I want only to inform you here and now that the light is on in the library as it was last night when we went to bed with orders not to disturb the Baron Klopstocks and their guest, and, furthermore, this morning the door is locked from the inside and there is no response."

"What's happened?" says Theo. "You know, my Clara has had dreams, terrible dreams. Have you knocked hard enough?"

Lister goes to the library door, tries the handle, shakes it, then knocks loudly. "Sir!" he says. "Madam!"

"We'd better break it down," says Theo, looking at the others one by one.

"I have orders not to disturb," Lister says. "We shall call the police."

"Clara will be frightened," says Theo.

"Tell her to confide in the police about her dreams, and get it off her chest," says Lister. "The more she says about her dreams when questioned, the better. As far as you two in the lodge are concerned we have been such stuff as dreams are made on all through the stormy night."

"There's a couple been wandering the grounds all night," says Theo. "They came in the car and I wouldn't let them out, as you ordered. Now they've lost the keys of the car and they're taking shelter under a tree. They look a suspicious pair to me."

"Forget them," says Mr. Samuel. "They're only extras."

"Better go back to Clara," says Lister. "It's nearly eight o'clock. See that the gates are opened."

"All right, Lister," says Theo in a hushed voice, looking towards the library. Then he departs quickly through the open door, mounts his bicycle and starts off up the drive. He gets drenched almost immediately for at that moment the storm descends with full concentration on the Klopstocks' country seat. Theo pedals vigorously, and rounding a bend he is forced to get off his bicycle and press forward on foot along the loud storm-darkened avenue, streaked every now and then as it is with a dart of lightning. On the way he passes a clump of elms under one of which, shrinking into the bark, are the couple of wandering friends from the car. Theo staggers onwards up the twisting drive and at the porch of his house lets fall the bicycle, bends through the torrent to the gates of the house, unlocks them and throws them open. Then he returns to the lodge and tumbles indoors.

Meanwhile the lightning, which strikes the clump of elms so that the two friends huddled there are killed instantly without pain, zig-zags across the lawns, illuminating the lily-pond and the sunken rose garden like a self-stricken flash-photographer, and like a zip-fastener ripped from its garment by a sexual maniac, it is flung slapdash across Lake Leman and back to skim the rooftops of the house, leaving intact, however, the well-insulated telephone wires which Lister, on the telephone to Geneva, has rather feared might break down.

Having alerted the police and quiveringly recommended an ambulance with attendant doctors and nurses, Lister now telephones to the discreet and well-appointed flat in Geneva which he prudently maintains, and extends a welcome to the four journalists who have been waiting up all night for the call, playing poker meanwhile, with the ash-trays piled high.

"Our four friends," Lister then instructs the household, "are to have first preference in anything you can say to them. They will, of course, have the scandal exclusives which Mr. Samuel and Mr. McGuire have prepared in the form of typescript, photographs and sound-recordings. The television, Associated Press and the local riff-raff are sure to question you wildly: answer likewise—say anything to them, just anything, but keep them happy. Isn't that right, Clovis?"

"Yes, the arrangements between our four special friends, ourselves, and our numbered accounts in the Swiss Trust Corporate can be left to Lister. We don't have any arrangements with the others. Keep them happy, that's all. For the television, throw your heads into your hands and sob, or display a sad disapproval of your late employers."

"I want to go to bed," says Heloise.

"I shall see that you are allowed to retire at the earliest possible moment, Heloise."

"Listen to Lister," says Eleanor.

Lister then books a telephone call to the residence of Count Rudolph Klopstock in Rio de Janeiro, and having done this, says to the others, "There's a delay to Brazil and they're five hours back. We should get the Count somewhere between four and five a.m. Rio time, and allowing for human nature on the telephone exchange between here and there the news will get around pretty quickly."

"The brother ought to know," says Eleanor.

"Know what?" says Lister.

"About the brother," says Eleanor.

"At the present moment," says Lister, "all we ourselves know is that the library door is locked with the Baron, the Baroness and their young friend unresponsive. We're justifiably apprehensive, that's all. Here comes the crime squad. Group yourselves apprehensively."

He opens the front door to the sound of sirens in the storm. Two police cars pull up at the door followed by an ambulance. An inspector of police, a police detective, two plain-clothes men, three uniformed policemen and a police photographer troop in the open door. The ambulance crew alight and come in out of the rain.

"This is the door, Inspector," says Lister, leading the way to the library.

The Inspector turns the handle, rattles it, bangs on the door and listens.

"Are you sure there's somebody inside?"

"We fear so. The light's still on as it was last night. The Baron gave orders they were not to be disturbed," Lister says. "I have already put through a call to the Baron's brother, as I felt it was right."

"Open the door," says the Inspector. Two hefty policemen break it down. The Inspector and his men crowd into the room. Lister follows while the rest of the household approaches the threshold. Mr. Samuel's camera clicks. Mr. McGuire has a small, light apparatus dangling from his wrist. The body of the Baroness is lying on the floor by the window in a large dark red stain. That of Victor Passerat lies curled against a bookcase which is well splashed with his blood. The Baron's body is slumped over a round table with a revolver not far from his fingers.

The women scream.

"Take the girls away," says the Inspector to a plain-clothes man. "Put them in the kitchen and make them calm down."

Clovis leads the way to the servants' quarters while the Inspector says to Lister, "Didn't you hear anything during the night? No shots? No shouting or screaming?"

The wind encircles the house and the shutters bang. From the attic comes a loud clatter. "No, Inspector. It was a wild night," says Lister.

Up the drive comes a caravan of cars.

The doctor has scrutinised the bodies, the police have taken their statements, they have examined and photographed the room. They have confiscated a letter written by the Baron, to the effect that he has just shot his wife and his secretary and is about to shoot himself, that this is the only solution and that he has no ill feelings against anyone. The Inspector has permitted Lister to read it but has refused it to the reporters who now swarm in the great hall and make a considerable hubbub.

The women have been released from the kitchen, having given their shaken and brief testimony, and again join the household group at the door of the library.

"I must have a last look," says Eleanor. Heloise casts a doleful eye at a television camera which does not fail to register it. The noise from the reporters swells as, one by one, the covered bodies on their stretchers are borne out of the room. "Here they come," says Lister to his troop, "Klopstock and barrel."

The bodies are stowed away in the ambulance. The police seal off the main quarters of the house, pushing the reporters out into the subsiding storm, and requesting the servants to retire to their wing.

The doctor then suggests he takes away the ladies to be treated for shock, but they bravely resist. "The porter's wife," says the Inspector, "could do with a bit of treatment. Better take her."

"I should take them both, sir," says Lister.

The reporters now crowd in the back door. "Inspector," says Lister, "I shall deal with them briefly then turn them out. We're all rather shaken. If you want any further information we are here."

"Very helpful," says the Inspector. "I'll leave a couple of my men to guard the house. Don't let anyone into the library or upstairs, any of you."

Heloise says, "They won't go upstairs, you can be sure of that. My Monet and my Goya are upstairs. One can't be too careful."

"I beg your pardon?" says the Inspector.

"She is overwrought," says Lister and says a word or two in the Inspector's ear.

"Yes, yes," says the Inspector, eyeing Heloise.

Lister murmurs another few words, gesturing towards the ceiling.

"Oh yes," says the Inspector, looking up. "We know about him. Relative of the Baroness."

"No, the Baron."

"Really? —Oh, well. An unfortunate family."

Lister adds a further piece of information in an undertone.

"Yes, well, if he's the father, you did the right thing," says the Inspector, anxious to join his men in the police car which is now waiting at the back door. He shoves his way through the crowd, refusing comment, and drives off.

Very soon Lister's four friendly journalists go to their car with their brief-cases under their arms, and drive away.

"Now for the riff-raff," Lister says to his clan. "Eleanor and Clovis can take one bunch in the sitting-room. Heloise and I will hold our press conference in the pantry. Hadrian and Irene can sit round the kitchen table with Pablo, representing the young approach. Mr. Samuel and Mr. McGuire—you can go the rounds."

They settle themselves accordingly. The cameras flash. Microphones are thrust forward to their mouths like hot-dogs being offered to hungry pilgrims.

The voices drown the hectic howl which descends from the breakfasting bridegroom.

Eleanor is saying, "Like a runaway horse, not going anywhere and without a rider."

Hadrian is saying, "The flight of the homosexuals . . ." to which his questioner, not having caught this comment through the noise, responds ". . . the flight of the bumble-bee?" "No," says Hadrian.

Lister is saying, ". . . and at one time in my youth I was a professional claque. I applauded for some of the most famous singers in the world. It was quite well paid, but of course, hand-clapping is an art, it's a question of timing. . . ."

"Togetherness . . ." says Irene.

Hadrian is saying, "Death is that sort of thing that you can't sleep off. . . ."

Pablo's voice cuts in, ". . . putting things in boxes. Squares, open cubes. It's a mentality. Framing them. . . ."

Eleanor says, "Like children playing at weddings and funerals. I have piped and ye have not danced, I have mourned and ye have not wept."

Lister, turning in his chair to a prober behind him, is saying, "He didn't do his own cooking or press his own trousers. Why should he have consorted, excuse my language, with his own wife?"

Clovis says, ". . . not on the typewriter—you wake the whole household, don't you? What I call midnight oil literature is only done by hand. It's an art. Yes, oh no, thanks, I intend to make other arrangements for publication."

Irene is saying, "No, he wanted it that way, I guess, until she did a Lady Chatterly on him. . . . A Victorian novel, don't you know it? She was really quite typical at heart when it came to Victor."

Lister is heard to recite, "For the thing which I greatly feared is come upon me, and that which I was afraid of is come upon me. I was out in safety, neither had I rest, neither was I quiet."

Eleanor is saying, "No. No living relatives on her side."

Pablo says, "Ghosts and fantasies rising from sex-repression."

Clovis says, "Descendant of the Crusaders."

". . . somewhat like the war horse," says Lister, "in the Book of Job: He saith among the trumpets Ha! ha! and he smelleth the battle afar off, the thunder of the captains and the shouting. . . ."

". . . hardly ever seen," Eleanor is saying. "He wears a one-piece suit zipped and locked. The Swiss invented the zip-fastener. . . ."

"Well it's like this," says Pablo, "if you put friendship out to usury and draw the interest . . ."

The Reverend has now come down for his breakfast and stands bewildered in the doorway of the servants' sitting-room where Eleanor and Clovis are holding their crowded conference. He has his press-cutting in his hand.

"Reverend!" says Eleanor, pushing over to him.

"There's a man on the landing outside my room. He made me come down the back stairs. Where's Cecil Klopstock? I want to show him this."

Eleanor is swept away and replaced by five reporters. "Reverend would you care to elaborate on your statement about the sex-drug . . . ? Did the Baron . . . ?"

Eleanor, herself surrounded once more, is saying, ". . . frothing and churning inside like a washing machine in full programme."

Lister, beside her, addresses another microphone. "The glories," he says, "of our blood and state

> Are shadows, not substantial things;
> There is no armour against fate;
> Death lays his icy hand on kings:
> Sceptre and crown
> Must tumble down,
> And in the dust be equal made
> With the poor crooked scythe and spade."

"Could you repeat that, sir?" says a voice. Clovis pushes his way through the mass of shoulders and reaches Lister. "Phone call from Brazil," he says. "The butler won't fetch Count Klopstock to the phone. Absolutely refuses. He's locked in the study with some friends and he's on no account to be disturbed."

"Leave word with the butler," says Lister, "that we have grave news and that we hope against hope to hear from the Count when morning dawns in Rio."

Hadrian is saying, "When my brother had the flower-stall at the Piazza del Popolo and Iolanda had a little pitch for the newspapers a few steps away . . . It was a windy corner."

The Reverend, though trembling, is eating his breakfast in bed. The storm has passed and the sun begins to show itself on the wet bushes, the wide green lawns and the sodden rose garden. The reporters with their microphones and cameras have trickled away. Lister is looking at the cigarette stubs on the floor. Clovis opens the kitchen window. A homely howl comes down from the attic.

A car approaches up the drive.

"No more," says Lister. "Send them away."

"It's Prince Eugene," says Eleanor. "He's gone round the front."

"Well, he'll be sent round the back," says Lister, kicking a few cigarette stubs under the sideboard. "Let us all go to bed."

Footsteps can be heard squelching round the back

of the house, and the top half of Prince Eugene's face appears at the open window.

"Have they all gone?" he says.

"It's our rest-hour, your Excellency."

"I'm a Highness."

Eleanor says, "Was there something we can do for you, your Highness?"

"A word. Let me in."

"Let his Highness in," says Lister.

Prince Eugene enters timidly. He says, "The neighbours have been parked out on the road all morning. They didn't have the courage to come. Admiral Meleager, the Baronne de Ventadour, Mrs. Dix Silver, Emil de Vega, and all the rest. Anyway, I got here first. Can I have one word with you, Lister, my good man?"

"Come into the office," says Lister, leading the way into the pantry office. Mr. Samuel's camera flicks imperceptibly, just in case.

Prince Eugene takes the chair indicated by Lister. "Any of you like to come over to my place? Have you thought it over? It's very comfortable. I can offer—"

"At the moment, sir," says Lister, "we want to go to sleep and we don't want to be disturbed."

"Oh, quite," says the Prince, rising. "It's only that I wanted to get here before the others."

"It's very understandable," says Lister, rising, too. "But in fact we've made our plans."

"Miss Barton? —Would she consider a few light household duties? Surely the poor fellow can't go on living here?"

"Miss Barton will be needed. Heloise desires her to stay. Heloise was a parlour maid but she married the new Baron early this morning."

"You don't say! They got married."

Lister whispers in his ear.

"Oh, I understand. Quite drastic, though, isn't it?"

"They can marry or not marry, as they please, these days, sir," says Lister. "Times have changed. Take Irene, for instance."

"Which one is Irene?"

"The very charming one. Quite the most attractive. A very good little cook, too."

"I can offer her a very good wage."

"These days," says Lister, "they want more." He again murmurs a few words in the Prince's ear.

"I'm not the marrying type," whispers the Prince shyly.

"It's the best I can offer, your Highness. She's happy enough with her evening off at the airport."

"Well, I'd better be going," says the Prince.

"Thank you for calling, sir."

Lister leads the way to the back door, where Prince Eugene hesitates and says, "Are you sure we can't make some alternative arrangement with Irene?"

"Yes," says Lister. "I have others in mind for her in this part of the world who would be grateful to have her seated at their table. She's a very capable young housekeeper. The Marquis of—"

"Very well, Lister. Arrange the details as soon as possible. Accept no other offers."

The Prince tramples round once more to the front of the house, gets into his car and is seen to be driven off, sunk in the back seat, pondering.

The plain-clothes man in the hall is dozing on a chair, waiting for the relief-man to come, as is also the plain-clothes man on the upstairs landing. The household is straggling up the backstairs to their beds. By noon they will be covered in the profound sleep of those who have kept faithful vigil all night, while outside the house the sunlight is laughing on the walls.